Fresh Horses

"Slocum?"

"Are you Beddoes?" Slocum asked.

"Josiah Beddoes, at your service," the heavier of the two men said. "My partner here's goin' to tote some water for them mules."

"Don't you want to take a look at the mules I brought?" Slocum asked as he swung out of the saddle.

"They look fine to me. Good, sturdy stock, by all appearances." Just then, Beddoes stepped inside a stall and reached for something out of sight.

"Look out," Tad yelled, as Beddoes leaned back out, a double-barreled shotgun aimed straight at Slocum. He heard the twin hammers click back and felt a rod of cold steel climb up his backbone. Instinctively, he ducked and clawed for the Peacemaker at his hip.

He saw a blur of movement out of the corner of his eye, and then the shotgun roared with an explosion of orange flame and a deadly swarm of lead shot that spewed toward him like a nest of angry hornets . . .

JAKE LOGAN

SHOOT-OUT AT WHISKEY SPRINGS

J

JOVE BOOKS, NEW YORK

JH

This is a work of fiction. Names, characters, places, and incidents either are the product of the author's imagination or are used fictitiously, and any resemblance to actual persons, living or dead, business establishments, events, or locales is entirely coincidental.

SHOOT-OUT AT WHISKEY SPRINGS

A Jove Book / published by arrangement with
the author

PRINTING HISTORY
Jove edition / April 2002

All rights reserved.
Copyright © 2002 by Penguin Putnam Inc.
This book, or parts thereof, may not be reproduced in any form
without permission.
For information address: The Berkley Publishing Group,
a division of Penguin Putnam Inc.,
375 Hudson Street, New York, New York 10014.

Visit our website at
www.penguinputnam.com

ISBN: 0-515-13280-2

A JOVE BOOK®
Jove Books are published by The Berkley Publishing Group,
a division of Penguin Putnam Inc.,
375 Hudson Street, New York, New York 10014.
JOVE and the "J" design
are trademarks belonging to Penguin Putnam Inc.

PRINTED IN THE UNITED STATES OF AMERICA

10 9 8 7 6 5 4 3 2 1

1

John Slocum heard a noise when he clamped his teeth together and knew it was the harsh grate of sand. He also knew he was long overdue for a drink and a good woman to share the soft bed he intended to fall into once he and Tad finished driving the herd of Missouri mules to Victor. He'd had enough of hard ground, rocks digging into his back and shoulder blades, enough of sand fleas and Mojave green rattlesnakes that hid in the shade of the yucca and the Joshua trees on the high desert.

"How much farther, Mr. Slocum?" Tad Foster called from the back of the mule herd for the fifteenth time that day, at least. Tad was a young wrangler he had picked up in Independence to help him drive the herd of twenty sound mules clear to California. Tad, short for Thaddeus, had said he was headed for California anyway. He had a sister, he said, in San Bernardino, which was just a day or two ride through Cajon Pass from Victor. Tad knew the way; he had been out here before, but it was all new country to Slocum—pretty as a postcard, but hotter than the hinges of hell in the daylight and cold as a well digger's sodden ass at night.

"You ought to know, Tad. I thought you had been this way before."

"Well, we come straight over from Yuma to San Bernardino, sir."

"Now you tell me," Slocum said, and his teeth grated on the grit in his dry mouth. If they had gone through Yuma, that would have added days to their travel time, and his contract called for him to deliver the mules to a man named Beddoes in Victor before the end of summer. And he was burning up July as it was. He had shed his black frock coat shortly after sunup that morning. It was tied down tight atop his bedroll, with the double-barreled Greener, its butt sticking out, just behind the cantle. He kept the 12-gauge Greener loaded with double-aught buck and it took hardly any time to slip it out of his bedroll in an emergency. At close range, the shotgun would cut a man in half and chew up what was left. He also carried a Colt Peacemaker on his belt, and in the boot under his right stirrup, his cherished Winchester '73 was within easy reach. In his boot, he carried a knife big enough to gut the biggest-bellied badman, and, for an ace in the hole, he had a little Remington belly gun nestled inside his shirt, held snug by his gun belt.

"Well, by my reckoning, Victor ought to be just a stone's throw over the next little rise, right where you see that lake dancing yonder."

"It does look like a lake," Foster said. "But I know it ain't."

"No, it's just another mirage, like all the rest we've been looking at for near a month."

"I'll be glad to get someplace," Foster said. "The bones in my butt feel like iron rods."

Slocum laughed. Tad was a good kid, and he had been pretty good company on the long ride from Missouri. But he could be a pest, too. He had wanted to stop in Barstow and rest up, which would have cost them at least another day. And while that was tempting, even to Slocum, business came first. Also, the mules were not taking the high desert all that well. Water holes were few and far between and he'd had to doctor a snakebite or two, and more than once, a mule had been spooked by the sudden jump-up of a jackrabbit hiding behind the spiky Spanish bayonets that littered the sandy desert.

"Well, I'll be glad to be shut of these here mules," Foster said, as if reading Slocum's mind. "They're all just about to go plumb loco in this danged heat."

"They aren't camels, you know."

"No, and I sometimes wished they was."

"No, boy, you don't," Slocum said. "There isn't a meaner pack animal on the face of the earth than a camel, be he of one hump or two."

"You know camels?"

"I've seen a couple," Slocum said. "The army brought a bunch over here to chase Apaches with, and it didn't work out."

"Apaches. You seen Apaches, too?"

"I reckon," Slocum said, and then he was standing up in the stirrups as he saw the top of a building through the shimmering glaze of the mirage. The big Palouse stud whickered as it smelled water and civilization. Slocum patted the horse's neck and settled back down in the saddle. "It won't be long now, boy," he said softly.

Slocum and Tad rode through the shimmering mirage, which evaporated into thin air and became hot sand once again. Below, the small town of Victor lay sprawled on both sides of the road, houses and buildings crowded together in the middle of nowhere, the roofs lit by the blazing sun. Slocum, with his keen eyes, spotted the maze of fences that marked the corrals of the stockyards at the north end of town and his heart picked up a beat. The Palouse wanted to break into a trot, but Slocum held the horse back. Unless he maintained control, the mules would follow dumbly and arrive with coats all sleeked with sweat, their lungs burning up with the dry, hot air.

"Yonder it lies, Mr. Slocum," Tad exclaimed.

"You keep those mules in check, Tad. Just ride in easy."

"Yes, sir," Tad said, and he mopped his brow with a bandanna and straightened the hat on his head as if he were going to a wedding.

Slocum could smell his own sweat and longed for a hot, soapy bath to wash away all the trail grit and grime while he puffed on a cheroot and let his tired muscles soak back to normal.

Slocum arrived first at the gate to the largest corral and leaned down and slipped the rope loose and opened it. "Just head 'em all in here, Tad," he said.

Tad crowded the mule in the lead so that it went toward the open gate, and Slocum rode up on the other side in case the leader spooked and didn't want to go inside the pole enclosure. Once the lead mule went in, the others followed and as they were milling around, Slocum swung the gate shut and retied the Manila rope that held it shut.

"Well, that's that," Tad said, grinning.

Slocum saw that there was a stock tank at the far corner of the corral. He didn't know if it had any water in it, but the lead mule started ambling that way, its ears perked to sharp cones, its rubbery nostrils twitching.

"Not quite, son. We have to look up Beddoes and get our money for these mules."

"Where do we do that?" Tad asked.

Slocum looked toward the livery stable and saw two men emerge into the sunlight. Both wore wide-brimmed, high-crowned hats that shadowed their faces. They both wore rough clothes, heavy duck pants, high-top work boots, and light chambray shirts. Neither appeared to be armed. At least neither was wearing a pistol. They looked like common laborers, Slocum thought—not farmers or cowmen, but practicing some other trade.

"Slocum?"

"Are you Beddoes?" Slocum replied.

"Josiah Beddoes, at your service," the heavier of the two men said. "And, this here's Vernon Deakins, my partner. Vern's goin' to tote some water for that tank. No use in letting the sun sop it all up. We'll get them mules watered right quick."

As if by silent command, Deakins went back inside the stable and emerged with two buckets. He walked over to a pump with a block and tackle dangling from a frame above it. He attached one of the buckets to a hook and lowered it into the well. Slocum heard the wooden bucket plop into water a long way down. Deakins started pulling the rope back up.

"Want some help? Foster here can fill that other bucket while Deakins is dumping that into the stock tank."

"No, Vern'll get it. You can water your horses inside here. Water's nice and cool in there."

"All right," Slocum said. He took off his hat and wiped the sweatband dry. He ran a hand through his thick black hair to dry his sweaty fingers and then put his hat back on. He rode over to the stables and Foster followed, swatting at flies that rose up from the dung piles to attack him.

Beddoes was a burly man, with narrow, rounded shoulders, no visible neck beneath the bandanna tied around it. He had brushy eyebrows and a yellowing moustache that dripped over his upper lip like moss. His pudgy lips were dry and cracked from the weather, and his hands were gnarled and cracked at the knuckles, showing signs of hard work. His face was florid, as if accustomed to taking strong drink or carrying too much weight for his short frame.

"Light down and come on inside," Beddoes said.

"Don't you want to take a look at the mules I brought?" Slocum asked as he swung out of the saddle.

"They look fine to me. Good, sturdy stock, by all appearances."

"They are fine-blooded stock," Slocum said, leading his horse into the stables. Foster dismounted and followed his employer, taking off his hat to swat at a swarm of bluebottle flies that swarmed up from a pile of old horse apples.

Beddoes disappeared inside the stable as Slocum walked toward him, leading the Palouse. When he went inside, Slocum squinted, trying to adjust his eyes to the dim light. Tad followed him in a moment later, his horse, a claybank mare, nudging him on as its nostrils distended at the smell of water.

"Right over yonder, gentlemen," Beddoes said, pointing to a barrel of water at the far end of the stable. Slocum stopped and motioned for Tad to go ahead since the mare was about to run away from the lad in her eagerness to get to the water.

Just then, Beddoes stepped inside a stall and reached for something out of sight.

"Look out!" Tad yelled, as Beddoes leaned back out, a double-barreled shotgun aimed straight at Slocum.

Slocum heard the twin hammers click back and felt a rod of cold steel climb up his backbone. Instinctively, he ducked, and clawed for the Peacemaker at his hip.

He saw a blur of movement out of the corner of his eye, and then the shotgun roared with an explosion of orange flame and a deadly swarm of lead shot that spewed toward him like a nest of angry hornets.

2

Slocum flinched as a hail of lead shot spanged against the wood of the stable and posts around him. He felt a sharp sting in his arm as young Tad fell against him, his body streaming blood from dozens of wounds.

"Get him, Vern," Beddoes yelled.

Slocum saw a shadow behind him, but before he could turn to face his attacker, he felt a crunching blow to his head. He slumped down, pain shooting through his head and darkness closing in on him. He fell, and Foster's body landed atop him just as the last pinpoint of light winked out in his brain.

"I got the bastid," Deakins said, panting. "Plumb cold-cocked him, that's for danged sure."

"I'll get those mules," Beddoes said, heading for the door. "Finish Slocum and that boy off with this."

Beddoes handed the shotgun to Deakins and put two shells in his hand.

"Do I gotta?" Deakins asked.

"Unless you want a witness, Vern."

Before Deakins could reply, Beddoes had left the stable and was outside in the corral. Deakins looked at the two men lying there. The boy was pretty badly shot up and Slocum was covered with blood, too. They both looked dead to Deakins. He turned his head away, and with shaking fingers, cracked open the shotgun. The empty shells ejected and he fumbled with the ones Beddoes had given him. He slid the cartridges into the breech and closed the barrels. He heard the mules braying outside as he cocked both hammers.

Deakins started to back away from the two men who had been shot to get another angle on them. Just then, the younger man moved and it appeared to Deakins that he was going to rise up.

"Hurry up in there, Vern," Beddoes called and Deakins jumped. Hastily he brought the shotgun up to his shoulder and touched off both barrels. He heard a groan and the sound of shot tearing into flesh and ripping into the wooden posts and walls of the stable. Without waiting to find out what damage he had done, Deakins ran outside.

"Hurry up," Beddoes said. "The whole town'll be down here in two seconds. Get our horses. Quick."

All of the mules were outside the corral and Deakins ran to the other side of the stable where two saddled horses were tied. He untied them, mounted one and led the other one out to Beddoes. The two men started driving the mules toward a dry wash that ran north and south and offered concealment from the small town of Victor. In moments they were out of sight, heading south. None in the town had seen them leave.

"Did you get both of 'em?" Beddoes asked when they were well away from the town.

"Yeah," Deakins answered.

"Kill 'em?"

"I gave 'em both barrels. Up close."

"Good. We'll cut east and head for Holcomb Valley. Looks to be we got clean away."

Deakins looked back to see if there was anyone on their back trail. Satisfied, he let out a sigh. There was no one following them.

When he looked over at Beddoes, the man was smiling. Gradually, Deakins's nerves began to calm and his hands stopped shaking.

"You want your shotgun back, Josiah?" Deakins asked.

"Yeah, gimme it."

The men rode on, driving the mules ahead of them as if they had all the time in the world.

Slocum swam upward through layers of darkness, in and out of bad dreams, and opened his eyes to a blurred figure hovering over him like some dark angel of death. He blinked and brought his vision into focus. When he did, he was staring into a pair of the most beautiful eyes he had ever seen.

He blinked again.

Then the pain in his back struck him as if someone had set fire to the soft bed he lay upon. He groaned and decided he was alive. He looked into the beautiful blue eyes and then saw the rest of her face, which was every bit as beautiful.

"Who are you?" Slocum asked, wincing with the sharp darts of pain that needled his back.

"My name is Lucille Bancroft. You can call me Lucy."

"I ought to call you 'Angel,' " he said. "I think you might have saved my life. Did you?"

"Someone did. That's for certain, mister. Luckily for you, Beddoes was using bird shot or you'd be in worse shape than you already are. I dug out a half-dozen pellets from your arm and more from your back and the rest that were in, ah, your backside."

"It wasn't Beddoes who shot me," Slocum said. "It was a feller named Deakins."

"Well, I wasn't the one who saved your life, either," Lucy said. "You have Curly Smithers to thank for that. He heard the shots and went running into the stables just as Beddoes and Deakins were riding off with a herd of mules."

"Mules they didn't pay one cent for."

"I don't know anything about that, but Curly had seen Beddoes with a shotgun earlier in the day and assumed he had used it on you."

"Where'd Beddoes go?" Slocum asked. "Do you know?"

Lucy smiled knowingly. She stared at him with those startling blue eyes and brushed aside a lock of honeyed hair that had fallen over her forehead. She had a pear-shaped face that was flawless, all peaches and cream, and full, inviting lips that begged to be kissed. Slocum felt a stirring in his loins despite the little stabs of pain in his back.

"I expect he's halfway to Holcomb Valley by now. With those mules he stole from you."

"You believe me, then," he said.

"Of course. Curly overheard Beddoes and Deakins talking about the mules before you and your friend even rode into town. He suspected they were going to steal them from you."

"Why didn't he say something? Tell the sheriff?"

Lucy laughed. "The sheriff? He was probably in on it with those two rascals."

"Why do you say that?" Slocum asked.

"Because Sheriff Weed used to be in cahoots with Beddoes and Deakins up in Holcomb Valley, some twenty years ago. They're thick as fleas."

"Weed?"

"Josiah Weed. You know him?"

"I know him for a thief and a murderer," Slocum said. "He and I tangled down in Texas once. About three years ago."

"Yes, he did leave for a while. Came back last year, ran for sheriff of Victor and won. In what some say was a crooked election."

"I'm not surprised."

Slocum thought back to that time when he had a run-in with Josiah Weed in Abilene. Weed had been posing as a Texas Ranger then, which allowed him to steal horses from unsuspecting ranchers. Slocum had seen to it that he had a short-lived career as a horse thief in Texas. But there were still ranchers down there who kept a rope handy for Weed if he ever returned. Horse thieves were still hanged in Texas and those ranchers had long memories.

"Where-where's Tad?" Slocum asked, struggling to lift himself up so that he could see the rest of the room. Lucy pushed him back down on his back.

"You just lie still, hear?" she said. "Is that your friend's name? Tad?"

"Tad Foster. Is he all right?"

"I don't think he'll make it," Lucy said. "He's lost a lot of blood."

"If Tad dies, Beddoes and Deakins will owe me a lot more than the price of the mules," Slocum said.

"You'd take an eye for an eye?" Lucy asked.

"No," Slocum said. "I'd take a life for a life."

"That could be dangerous. You've already made a few enemies here in Victor."

"I don't know anyone in Victor. In fact, I've never been here before."

"Is your name John Slocum?" she asked.

"Maybe. Why?"

"If it is, your reputation has preceded you. From what Curly tells me, you're a troublemaker, a man who sticks his nose where it doesn't belong. In fact, one of the ladies at the Desert Watering Hole, a local gambling house and drinking parlor here, says that your nose isn't the only thing you stick where it doesn't belong."

"I wonder what she meant by that," Slocum said.

"Yes," Lucy said. "I wonder, too."

Slocum let it pass. His mind was on other matters just then. The pain in his back was receding somewhat and the longer he stayed here, the farther away those stolen mules were getting.

"Now, let's change the subject, Lucy. Where is Holcomb Valley and why would Beddoes and Deakins steal those mules and try to kill me and the boy?"

"A few years ago, a man named William Holcomb was exploring that valley up there. He was attacked by a grizzly bear and shot it. And, he found gold, lots of it. There was a gold rush up in the San Bernardino Mountains.

They built a town and named it after Holcomb's daughter, Belle. They called it Belleville."

"I think I heard of that," Slocum said.

"Gradually, the gold petered out, some said. Others say there's a lake of gold underneath the valley, the so-called Mother Lode. Most of the prospectors left or died, but a few stayed on. Those who stayed kept silent, but some still watch that assay office in San Bernardino, looking for someone to stake a big claim. Beddoes and Deakins are two sneaks who work for a man who owns a lot of mines up in Holcomb Valley, a mystery man who moved there less than a year ago and started buying up claims and staking new ones. And, it was shortly after this man arrived that the killings started."

"Killings?"

"Murders, Mr. Slocum. Unsolved murders. And, and . . ."

Lucy began to sob then and mutter something Slocum couldn't hear.

"And then what?" he asked softly.

Lucy dabbed at her eyes with a kerchief she had tucked inside her sleeve and drew in a deep breath to compose herself. She looked into Slocum's eyes and he could see the pain and anguish in their depths.

"And then, two weeks ago, my father was murdered. Like the others."

"And do you think Beddoes and Deakins had something to do with it?"

"I don't know. I'm sure Beddoes was involved. But, my father wasn't killed with a shotgun."

"How did he die?" Slocum asked.

Lucy choked on the question and it took her a few

seconds to recover. "He was dragged to death behind a horse. He had a rope tied around his neck. He died a slow, agonizing death."

She shuddered at the recollection and Slocum's heart went out to her. It sounded to him that whoever killed her father didn't just want to murder him. The killer wanted to send a message.

But why?

Slocum opened his mouth to ask another question, but just then they heard a commotion in the room next door. Then they heard footsteps pounding on the hallway floor outside Slocum's room. The door burst open and a man, his face drained of blood, cried out.

"Miss Lucy!"

"What is it, Curly?"

"Come quick. I think that boy's dying."

Slocum beat Lucy to the door, despite the pain that shot through his arms and back. The man who had come in got out of his way just in time.

3

Slocum strode through the open door to Tad Foster's room. A thin, gray-haired man stood next to the bed near the window, holding Tad's bloody wrist in his hand. Slocum went to the wounded man and looked down at his face.

"Are you the sawbones?" Slocum asked the man with the startled look on his face.

"I'm Doc Wilkins. And you must be John Slocum. The boy's been asking for you."

"He's alive, then."

"Just barely. Hanging on by a thread."

"Tad, Tad?" Slocum called, picking up Tad's other hand, which lay limp at his side. "Can you hear me?"

"Easy now, Slocum," Wilkins said.

"Keep him alive," Slocum husked as he squeezed Tad's hand.

"You look as if you might need some medical attention yourself," the doctor said.

"Never mind me. Just keep Tad alive."

The doctor shook his head, but bent over the bed and placed his ear against the young man's chest. He listened for a few seconds, then stood up straight.

"His heart's giving out. The beat is very weak and erratic."

"Is he bleeding to death?" Slocum asked as Lucy and Curly quietly entered the room. They stood well away from the bed, watching in silence.

Foster's eyelids quivered as if he was struggling to lift them up with sheer willpower. Then, they fluttered and his eyes opened. Slocum squeezed Tad's hand. "Hold on," he said.

"Ma?" Foster said. "Ma, it hurts."

"You're going to make it, Tad."

"John, that you?"

"It's me, Tad. I'm here."

"I-I can't see too good."

Slocum looked up at the doctor, who shook his head.

"That's good, Tad. You hang on, hear?"

"I'm startin' to feel numb all over," Tad said. "Like I'm floating."

Slocum heard a sob and knew it had come from Lucy. He did not turn to look at her, but stared down at Tad. He knew the young man was dying. He had seen enough men his age die in the War between the States. His stomach knotted up with the memories. Some of those killed were no more than boys, with faces like Tad's. After Pickett's ill-fated charge at Gettysburg, where Slocum was a sharpshooter, he had seen many such men strewn across the battlefield, many still wet behind the ears. His jaw turned to granite as he clenched his teeth.

"Stay with it, Tad," Slocum husked, but he did not need to look at the doctor to know Tad was slipping away.

"He lost a lot of blood," the doctor said softly. "I'm sorry."

"I know," Slocum said. "I'm sorry, too. And someone's going to be a lot sorrier if this man dies."

The doctor coughed, cleared his throat. He cocked his head and placed his ear on Tad's chest once again and listened for several seconds. "His heart is growing weaker," he said. "I'm afraid he doesn't have long now. I gave him some laudanum for the pain. That's all I can do. He's bleeding internally."

"I figured that," Slocum said. "Those lead pellets play hob with a man's innards."

"You were in the war?" the doctor asked.

Slocum didn't answer, but his jaw tightened again and a muscle rippled just under his chin. Yes, he had seen men torn up inside, opened up like airtights by the field surgeons to expose the carnage a minié ball caused a man's vital organs. It was better if a lead ball went clean through, but often the soft lead flattened on bone or sheared off and splintered, piercing lungs, liver, gall bladder, spleen, kidneys. He could well imagine how Tad's insides must look, even with the smaller bird shot tearing through his young flesh.

Tad's eyelids fluttered again, but his eyes did not open for several seconds. "Hold on," Slocum said, in a gruff whisper that was almost like a prayer.

Then Tad's eyes opened and Slocum saw that they were cloudy with pain, no longer bright, no longer shining. Then, his eyes filmed over with a frosty glaze. He half-raised himself, struggling for one last breath, but then his body turned rigid. He opened his mouth, but no sound came out and he fell back down. There was a rattling sound in his throat. His eyes closed and stayed shut. His body gave a final shudder and then he was still.

"He's gone," the doctor said. When he saw Slocum's hard stare, he leaned over one more time and listened for a heartbeat. "Yes," he said. "His heart has stopped."

"Is there someone in town who can see to his burial?" Slocum asked. "I'll pay whatever it costs."

"I'll arrange it," Wilkins said. "It won't cost much, but we have a cemetery east of town."

"Thanks," Slocum said, just before the room started to spin around. He reached out to grab the bed, but staggered away from it, suddenly weak, his legs turning to rubber.

"Better get him back to bed, Lucy," Wilkins said. "Curly, give her a hand."

Slocum tried to shake them off, but Lucy grabbed his left arm and held on tightly, while Curly clasped the other. They led him out of the room where Tad had died and led him to the bed in the adjoining room.

Slocum tried to fight them off once more, but the room teetered on an invisible fulcrum and he crashed onto the bed, tumbling into a deep darkness from which there was no escape.

Hours later, Slocum awoke with a dry throat and a bewilderment toward his surroundings. The room was dark, but there was a lamp burning on a table near the bed. The soft yellow light threw long shadows on the walls and floors.

"You're awake," Lucy said.

"Whe-where am I?"

"In the same bed you were in before," Lucy replied. "Don't you remember?"

Slocum glanced around. The room looked different in the dark, but he decided it was the same room he had been in before he lost consciousness. Little darts of pain peppered his back and arms when he moved. He flexed his hands and stretched his legs. He guessed that all the essential parts of him were still working.

"Yeah, I guess I must have passed out."

"You did. I was very worried. Curly helped me get you into bed."

Slocum realized then that he was naked under the flimsy bedsheet. He looked sharply at Lucy. "Did someone steal my clothes?"

Even in the low light, Slocum could see that Lucy was blushing. The flush to her cheeks made her look even more beautiful in the lamplight. He felt a tug at his loins and that was further confirmation that he was still essentially sound in body and mind.

"Tad?" Slocum asked, a husky rasp in his voice.

"Your friend passed on, I'm afraid. He was just too badly wounded."

Slocum closed his eyes and let his last memories of Tad Foster parade across his mind. He opened them again when Lucy placed her hand atop his in a comforting gesture of sympathy. "I'm sorry," she said.

"He was a good man."

"Yes. I'm sure he was."

She started to take her hand away, but Slocum reached up and clasped it in his. "That feels good," he said. "Thanks."

"I wish there were more I could have done. More the doctor could have done."

"You both did all you could, Lucy."

"You must be hungry. Are you?"

"I could eat," Slocum said. "But first, I want you to tell me more about the death of your father and how Beddoes might figure into it."

"Are you willing to go back with me to Holcomb Valley?" she asked.

"If that's where Beddoes and Deakins are headed."

"I'm sure they are. Just as sure as they had something to do with my father's death. I'll help you all I can. I want to see my father's killers brought to justice and I know the law's not going to do it. Will you help me?"

"I will, if I can," Slocum said.

He could see her face beaming in the lamplight. She smiled and her even, white teeth were dazzling even in the dimness. He had not had a woman in a long time, and Lucy was not only becoming but he suspected she harbored a lustiness that had never been tapped before. Her breasts swelled beneath her dress when she leaned close to him and he squeezed her hand to let her know that he wanted her.

"I want to see if that girl in the saloon was right about you," she said. "If she was, I want to seal our bargain with a kiss."

Her lips were very close and he could smell her perfume, the female musk of her. It was a heady aroma and made him forget his flesh wounds.

"Just a kiss?" he husked.

"That's as far as I go, Mr. Slocum. I'm saving myself for marriage."

"If might be better, and more sure, if you saved your money for marriage," Slocum said. "Experience is worth any number of virgins on the marriage bed."

"Oh, is that so?" Lucy snapped, blushing radiantly.

"Ask the gal in the saloon," he said, taking her into his arms and kissing her passionately.

Lucy sighed deeply and he felt her breasts quiver against his bare chest, the nipples hardening to kernels as he clamped her to his body.

He broke the kiss and she let out a deep sigh. Her eyelids fluttered as if she was about to swoon. He held onto her arms in case she fainted, but then her eyes opened wide and she took in a deep breath.

"My." She sighed. "I didn't know it would be like this," she said.

"Like what?"

"I-I'm-I feel like I'm on fire inside. Deep inside."

"Maybe you are."

"Yes, yes, maybe I am. Maybe you ignited something in me that I didn't know was there."

"Was the kiss good enough for you?" he asked.

She leaned toward him and closed her eyes as she brushed his lips with hers. He kissed her again, and this time she gave back as much as he gave. He felt his loins blaze with heat. Then, she put a hand in his lap and tugged at his manhood, which was already turning hard, and it leaped to life in her hand and throbbed as she squeezed it tightly.

"Take me, John Slocum," she breathed. "Take me, now."

He felt the heat of her breath on his face as he turned her around to lay her on the bed. And still she gripped him as though unwilling to let him go before he finished what she wanted him to do.

4

Lucy slipped out of her clothes with Slocum's expert help and her willing hands. He helped with the back buttons on her blouse and when he slid the garment from her shoulders, she seemed to writhe with pleasure as the lamplight smudged each breast with a touch of orange rouge. He leaned over and kissed her in the hollow just below her left shoulder blade and she moaned low in her throat.

"You won't be rough, will you?" she asked, her voice so low he could barely hear it.

"Is this your first time?"

"Yes. And I'm scared."

"Just relax, Lucy. Enjoy the moment. I'll go slow and I'll lead you. All you have to do is follow."

"I want you to go slow. You're hurt."

"Don't worry. I won't bleed on you. The soreness will go away, just like your fear."

"Umm," she moaned as he lay her gently on her back and rose above her. She touched his chest with her hands and he smiled down at her. Then he reached down be-

tween her legs and began to rub the thatched mound. She
began to undulate with the rhythm of his kneading and
she made little cooing sounds.

"That-that feels so good," she said.

"It will feel much better soon," Slocum promised.

He slipped his middle finger just inside her cunt and
she quivered at the touch. Gently, he began to move his
finger in and out, stroking the silken lining of her cunt
until it grew hot and ran with warm fluids that prepared
her for what was to come.

When he touched her clit with the tip of his finger, she
jumped beneath him as if an electric charge had shot
through her body. "Oh, oh," she cried, and as he continued to stroke the little love button, her hips began to rise
and fall in unison with his own tempo.

He slid up her body until his prick touched her just
above her soft, wet mound. She grasped him tightly and
let out a long sigh. He continued to finger her until she
cried out for him to enter her. "Oh, John, I want you,"
she whispered. "Inside me. Quick. Now."

Slocum eased himself down and touched the portals of
her cunt with the tip of his prick. She quivered beneath
him in anticipation. "There, there," she breathed. "Yes.
Yes."

Slocum removed his hand and caressed one of her
breasts as he slowly dipped his hips to enter her. Lucy
stiffened for a moment when the tip of his prick slid past
her lips, then relaxed as he withdrew partially. He took it
slow and easy, plumbing just inside her until her fingernails dug into the small of his back and she slid her hands
down to his buttocks and pulled him down hard against
her loins. He pushed deeper and she sighed with pleasure.

Then he withdrew again, but did not pull his prick out all the way. He moved from side to side and she moaned with desire. She pulled on his buttocks again and again he pushed into her, deeper this time. Her mouth opened and her eyes closed as he held steady and waited another moment.

"It-it feels good," she said. "I want you to go deeper. Deep inside me."

"It might hurt a little," he said. "You're a virgin I see."

"I don't care. Tear it out. Whatever's there. I want it all, John."

Slocum took in a deep breath, then plunged deeper until the tip of his prick struck her maidenhead. He felt it give as he stroked back and forth, gently, to loosen its bonds.

"Yes, yes," she whispered, and the sounds were low in her throat, almost like a cat purring.

Slocum pushed through the maidenhead and Lucy gasped, stiffened for just a second, then he was in deep and she began to thrust her hips upward, impaling him even deeper inside her. He met her every upthrust with a downthrust of his own and soon they were in perfect rhythm, the bed slats creaking with their lusty thrashing.

Slocum paced himself and he was rewarded when Lucy cried out as a sudden orgasm shuddered through her loins. Then she screamed as he thrust deeper, plumbing to the very core of her cunt with his swollen prick. She screamed and clutched him tightly, her fingernails digging into the small of his back. But Slocum felt no pain, and when her scream subsided into a low moaning sound of pleasure, he withdrew partially to let their emotions settle down. He held there, motionless, the head of his prick just inside the opening folds of her cunt and she sighed deeply and looked up at him for a long moment.

"That was the most delightful feeling I've ever had in my life," she said.

"It can feel even better," Slocum promised.

"I can't believe it."

Then she thrust her hips upward and he sank deep inside her again. She cried out once more as she reached one climax, then another and another until her skin was sleek with sweat and she thrashed beneath him in a mindless paroxysm of pleasure.

"Yes, oh, yes," she screamed and Slocum smiled with approval.

He did not feel much pain, not the deep kind of pain that a serious injury would have caused. He felt as if he was being pricked with needles or knifepoints where the lead shot had torn through his flesh. But he knew, just from the feel, that the wounds were not deep. He had been lucky. Poor Tad had caught the brunt of Beddoes's cowardly attack, and he had paid the price. But, he vowed, Tad's death would be avenged, even if it cost him his own life.

Slocum brushed away thoughts of himself and his friend. Lucy was steaming beneath him, blazing with a desire that had not been quenched with the ferocity of her orgasms. She was a woman now, a woman who had surrendered her virginity and given her body up for pleasure.

"Are you satisfied yet?" he asked. "Are you happy?"

"I'm happy," she said softly. "But don't know if I will ever be satisfied. I never knew there could be so much pleasure in this life. I never knew my body could sing with such joy."

"That's the way it should be, Lucy."

"I wish someone had told me before how good it would be."

"This is one of life's biggest secrets."

"I know. Now."

He sank into her and her body bucked and shivered as he ravished the deepest part of her cunt. She thrashed beneath him and dug her fingers into his back as if she were holding on for dear life.

And then, she screamed again, as her body shuddered in the throes of still another climax. Now, he held on to her and covered her body with his, pinning her to the shaking bed with its wooden slats that creaked with their weight.

"Oh, we're making so much noise," she said. "Someone will hear us."

"Do you hear that wind out there?" Slocum asked. "It's making more racket than we are."

It was true. The desert wind had come up and was blowing hard against the weathered boards of the hotel. Lucy listened for a moment, then laughed softly. "You're right," she said. "I hadn't even heard it before. No wonder. I was too busy listening to the pounding of my heart."

Slocum took her to the heights once again and then she began begging him to scale the mountain of pleasure with her. "You haven't thought of yourself," she said. "I know you want pleasure, too."

"Whenever you're ready," he said. "A man only gets one shot and it takes a while to reload."

"I know," she said. "My mother told me often enough. But I want you to come, John. Come with me."

"That," he said, "will be my pleasure."

Slocum bent to his task with all the skill of a great lover. He slid his cock in and out of Lucy's cunt with slow, sure strokes, playing her as a maestro would play a violin. He tantalized her and she responded with a willingness that almost surprised him. She arched her back and he ran a hand down one of her legs, over the smooth skin, and she cried out and thrashed beneath him as if she were an animal caught in a trap, struggling to free itself. But Lucy did not want to be freed. She clasped his buttocks with both hands and held him prisoner until he began to increase the speed of his strokes. He plumbed her steamy depths faster and faster until she screamed in his ear. Then he raced with her to the very top of the peak they both desired and she let out a series of whoops and scratched his back and pulled his long black hair as she writhed in the throes of a massive orgasm.

Slocum emptied his balls inside her and knew she could feel the hot juices fill her, because she became breathless and voiceless and quivered like a freezing bird in his grasp.

"Yes, oh, yes, John, you did it," she purred. "And it was wonderful. So beautiful. Thank you, thank you."

"Thank you," he said, breaking into a smile.

He lay atop her until both their hearts stopped pounding and then he slid from her belly and lay beside her, aching for one of the cheroots he knew had to be somewhere in the room.

"Do you know where my smokes are?" Slocum asked.

"Those ugly little cigars?"

"They don't smoke ugly."

"I know where they are," she said.

"I'm dying for a smoke."

"Still not satisfied?" she said, a mocking tone in her voice.

"I reckon I'm as satisfied as you are, Lucy. Would you mind if I had a little extra pleasure? A smoke would calm me down some and might make me ready to go again."

"I'll get you one of your cigars," she said, slipping out of the bed.

"Cheroots," Slocum corrected.

"Well, at least the name for them is pretty."

She brought him a cheroot and a small box of lucifers. Slocum bit off a small portion of the end and spat it out on the floor as Lucy climbed back into bed. He struck the match and lit the cheroot, drawing the satisfying smoke into his mouth and lungs.

"It doesn't smell as bad as a cigar," Lucy said.

"They're not to everyone's taste, but I've become accustomed to them."

"I want you again," she said.

"Now?"

"When you're ready. I've got something to tell you first, though."

"What's that?"

Lucy sighed and reached a hand out to lay it across Slocum's flat belly. "I-I've tried to block it out of my mind," she said. "But this, this loving with you brought it all back up and I can't just keep holding it all inside."

"If it will make you feel any better," Slocum said, "go ahead. Let it out. Say what you have to say."

"I-I'll try," she said, and then Slocum heard a sob. When he looked at her, even in the dimness of the room, he could see that she was crying. "When I told you my father was killed, I left out some of it."

"What did you leave out?" His voice was very gentle and Lucy dried the tears on her face with a swipe from the back of her other hand.

"My father wasn't the only one who was murdered up in Holcomb Valley," she said. "My fiancé, the man I was planning to marry, Robert Magill, was killed, too. He-he was with my father. I don't think, at least I don't want to think, that he was meant to be murdered like that. They-they didn't drag him like they did my father. They just left him by the road. But they made sure he couldn't talk about my father's murder."

"What do you mean?" Slocum asked.

"They-they shot him in the head. At close range."

"I'm sorry," Slocum said.

"What I feel badly about was that Robert had asked me-had asked me to-to . . ."

"To what?"

"To do what we did just now. And I told him I wanted to save myself for marriage. I wanted him to marry a virgin."

"And now you regret it."

"I-I did. I think that's why I wanted you to . . . to bed me."

"I don't understand," he said.

"Don't you?" She rose up and put her arms around Slocum and then kissed him hard on the lips. "Don't you?" she whispered.

Then she released him and began sobbing again. He reached over and patted her on the shoulder.

"I-I thought," she said, "that if I refused you and you were killed, then I'd miss another chance at love, at being loved. I know it's shameless of me, but I kept thinking about Robert and how selfish I was to deny him my body when he wanted it so. Do you understand now?"

"Yes," Slocum said softly. "I understand."

5

When Slocum awoke in the morning, he discovered that Lucy had sent his clothes out to be washed and had brought breakfast up on a tray.

"How did you manage that?" he asked.

"The breakfast?"

"No, getting my clothes washed so quick."

"I washed them and the wind dried them . . . almost. I ironed them and they should be fully dried by the time you put them on."

"Thanks for leaving me the cheroots and the matches."

"I didn't fix your breakfast. I had the hotel cook do it."

"You're mighty nice to me," Slocum said.

"You've been nice to me, too. I wondered, though, if you wanted to stay and say some words over your friend. I arranged for him to be buried today."

"I want to get after those mules. There's nothing more I can do for Tad."

"That's what I thought," she said. "I'm taking you to Holcomb Valley, of course."

"You are? That's mighty nice of you."

"I have a stake in what happens when you get there, you know. Beddoes and Deakins work for the man who murdered my father and my betrothed."

"And who is that?"

"I'm not exactly sure, of course, but I have strong suspicions that my father was murdered by a man named Lucas Chadwick. He's a very mean man and he's powerful. And greedy."

"Can you prove Chadwick killed your father?"

"No," she said. "Not yet, anyway. But I know he's responsible. I-I . . ."

"What?"

"I was hoping you'd help me. Once you get up to Holcomb Valley and see how bad things are there, I feel sure you could find out the truth about my father's death."

"I'm not a detective," Slocum said.

"No, but you're smart and you have a stake in this now. Beddoes works for Luke Chadwick. I'm sure that Chadwick ordered him to steal your mules and murder you."

"Well, Beddoes and his henchman, Deakins, are going to pay for what they did to Tad Foster."

"Chadwick will try and kill you, too," she said.

Slocum began to put on his clothes. He pulled aside the shade and saw that it was still dark outside. But he could see that the sky was turning pale and some of the stars had already winked out.

"Then," Slocum said, "I may well get right in the middle of your troubles, Lucy. But I won't go out of my way to look for trouble. I want you to understand that."

"No. I understand. And I wouldn't expect you to. It's

just that Holcomb Valley has become a den of thieves—
and murderers."

"Do you have a horse?" Slocum asked suddenly.

"Why, yes. I rode my horse down here to Victor."

"Then let's go saddle up and get on up to Holcomb
Valley. Where are my saddlebags and gear?"

"Downstairs, at the hotel desk. But, John, I-I don't
think it's going to be easy for us to leave town."

Slocum finished strapping on his gun belt and slipped
the little Remington belly gun inside his shirt. He checked
the bowie knife to see that it was snug in its scabbard
inside his boot. He pulled the Colt Peacemaker from its
holster and spun the cylinder. He saw that all the cham-
bers were full. He slid the cylinder slightly and put the
hammer on safety cock. Some men, he knew, always left
one cylinder empty and put the hammer on that cylinder
so they wouldn't shoot themselves in the foot. But Slocum
liked to have all six bullets ready. There was no telling
when that sixth cartridge would be needed in a shoot-out.

"Beddoes and Deakins have friends here in Victor,"
Lucy said, as Slocum started for the door. "We have to
be careful. They might try and stop us."

"Let's hope they're still asleep," Slocum said, as he
lifted the latch to open the door.

"That's why I got up early to do the washing and mend-
ing."

"Well, the cook must have been up. Who else?"

"Just Curly. He helped me."

"Do you trust him?"

"Yes, of course. Why do you ask?"

"It seems to me that Curly is always around. Right
handy."

"I've always found Curly to be trustworthy," she said defensively.

"I hope he isn't a talker," Slocum said.

"What do you mean?"

"Someone who goes around jabbering everything he knows to every who'll listen."

"Well, I don't know about that."

"He told you about Beddoes and Deakins, didn't he?"

"Yes, but I was following those men to see what they were up to."

"Did you know about the mules?"

"Yes, I did. Belleville is a small town. People talk. I knew Luke needed mules for his mining operations and that he was sending Beddoes and Deakins to Victor to pick them up."

"Did you know I was bringing them?"

Lucy's face blanched, then turned pink as the blood rushed back in a becoming blush.

"Yes. You're quite notorious, even in Holcomb Valley."

"I see," Slocum said, then opened the door. He stopped then and turned to Lucy. "My bedroll?"

"It's in the stable. I didn't think you'd need it here in the hotel."

"What about the shotgun that was rolled up in it?"

"The clerk down at the desk has it in a safe place."

"Looks to me as if you've thought of everything," he said.

"I tried," Lucy said, and Slocum could see that she was peeved by all his questions.

"Let's go, then," he said and stepped through the doorway. He looked both ways down the hall, his right hand dangling close to the butt of his Colt .45. He walked to the stairs, with Lucy following him, and listened to the boards creak underfoot. Down at the desk, a sleepy clerk of an indeterminate age, but with pork-chop whiskers that were white tipped and a dripping moustache that looked dyed, brought him his shotgun.

"Anybody been hanging around the hotel lobby?" Slocum asked.

"Nope. But I seen somebody skulkin' by across the street. Headin' for the stables."

"You're a good man," Slocum said. "How long ago was that?"

"Oh, less'n fifteen minutes ago, I'd say. My name's Scott, Mr. Slocum. Scott Lambert."

"I supposed you've heard of me, too," Slocum said, trying to conceal his sarcasm.

"Well, yep, I reckon so. I was with the Calhoun County militia out of Georgia. Fought with your pa at Manassas, which they now call Bull Run."

"Well, I'll be damned," Slocum said.

"Yep. Your pa used to talk about you all the time. And, I knew your brother, Robert, too. He talked about you likewise."

"I thought I recognized that Georgia drawl when you first spoke," Slocum said, extending his hand. "Nice to meet a Georgia boy way out here."

"I caught a minié ball at Manassas. Never did know what happened to the Slocums, your pa and brother. I missed the rest of the war. Ball plumb splintered my leg and I walk on wood now and pack a cane for balance."

"My pa, William, was killed at Manassas by one of those minié balls like the one that caught you."

"And Robert, your older brother? He was just a kid when I knew him. But I wasn't much older myself."

"Robert fought with Stonewall Jackson, who got that name at Manassas, if you remember. He made lieutenant and then got killed in a charge led by old Stonewall. I always thought Jackson got my brother killed because he was so damned fearless."

"Could be. Manassas was one bloody fight, I can tell you that."

"Don't you miss the Alleghenies, old-timer?" Slocum asked.

"I would if I hadn't gone there and seen for myself what happened in them hills after the war, the damned carpetbaggers and all. We were sold out, plumb sold out."

"Yes," Slocum said softly, "I know."

"John, we'd best hurry," Lucy said, tugging on his arm.

"I got your bedroll back here, too," the clerk said. "I reckon you want that."

"Yeah, might come in handy," Slocum said, taking the bedroll from the old Civil War veteran. "Thanks. Be seein' you."

"I surely hope so, Mr. Slocum. You watch your back, hear?"

"I will," Slocum said.

Slocum and Lucy stepped outside the hotel. The pre-dawn air was chilly and the street was deserted, or seemed to be. Slocum stopped and looked both ways as Lucy waited a half step behind him. She carried only a small carpetbag and was dressed for riding in a long skirt, boots, a chambray blouse and a light blue jacket that did little to ward off the cold, but was very becoming on her. Slocum wore his freshly dusted and ironed black frock coat, which acted as a windbreaker even in the slightest breeze.

"It looks clear," Slocum said. "Stable down that way?" He nodded to the right.

"Yes, it's at the end of this street. I'm wondering, though, if we shouldn't walk over another street and come in the back way. There are two entrances to the stables."

"You think somebody might be waiting for us on this street?"

"I don't know," she said. "But they might not expect us to come in the back way."

"Good idea," Slocum said. "Better to be safe than sorry."

At the far end of the street, a cur slunk across the open, its tail between its legs. It came from the direction of the stables and Slocum wondered if someone had kicked it out of its bed. The dog disappeared and there was a silence in the street that was deep, as if the town were holding its breath, waiting for something to happen.

Lucy led Slocum across to the other side of the street, walking quickly and glancing both ways as if she were fearful of something emerging out of the darkness. They went between two clapboard buildings that were weathered by the wind, and the stars overhead looked very bright even as the sky began to pale. The moon had long since set, Slocum decided, as they emerged on the next street, which was not as wide as the other one and even darker, if that was possible. And quieter.

"The stables are beyond the next block of buildings," Lucy said. "It's awful quiet."

"Yes, I know," Slocum said. "Too damned quiet, if you ask me. Doesn't anyone get up early in this town?"

"Usually some of the storekeepers are sweeping the

boardwalk by now," she said. "It's strange."

"Yeah, mighty strange."

Slocum said no more as they walked at a brisk pace up the street, staying off the boardwalk so they wouldn't make any noise. He kept one hand close to his pistol butt, ready to draw at a moment's notice.

When they reached the stables, Slocum turned to Lucy and held up his hand. "You'd better wait outside while I go inside and check things out."

"All right," Lucy said.

Slocum set down his bedroll and the sawed-off Greener shotgun. He stepped inside the dark stables and heard his horse whicker. He stayed to the deeper shadows and walked down the line of stalls until he saw his horse, the Palouse, its head outside the stall door. He rubbed its nose and then went to the next stall and saw Tad's horse. He spoke to it, calling the claybank mare by its name. "Hello, Sugar. You ready for a ride?"

Sugar whinnied low and Slocum slipped the bridle from a peg on the outside of the stall, opened the gate and stepped inside. He slipped the halter over the mare's head and buckled the chin strap, then led the horse from the stall.

Just as he was about to step outside at the back, he heard a noise behind him. He went into a fighting crouch and turned quickly, reaching for his pistol.

A man stood at the far end of the stable, in silhouette. Slocum could not see his face, nor could he tell if the man was armed.

"Where in hell do you think you're going?" the man asked.

And at that moment, Slocum knew that it was no accident that the man was there. The hackles on the back of his neck stiffened and he felt a cold chill crawl up his spine as if he had been touched by the hand of Death itself.

6

Slocum slapped Sugar on the rump and whirled to face the man at the other end of the stable. He sidestepped, but stayed in a fighting crouch, his right hand hovering just above the butt of his Colt pistol.

"Where in hell do you think you're goin'?" the man asked again, his figure still in shadow. He was standing just past the tack room at the left of the stables, and the tack room door was closed almost all the way.

"I don't believe that's any of your business, mister," Slocum said, his voice laced with steel.

Out of the corner of his eye, Slocum saw Lucy step into view, outside the stable. She held Sugar by the reins.

"Well, I'm makin' it my business. Beddoes is a friend of mine, and so is Deakins. And they won't like you goin' after them with that woman."

"Beddoes killed a friend of mine," Slocum said. "He owes me a life he took. Do you want to buy into that?"

"You ain't goin' no damn place, Slocum. Least of all with that troublemakin' woman."

"Lucy, get out of the way," Slocum said. He did not know whether she moved or not, but he hoped she was out of the line of fire, because he knew there was bound to be gunplay.

Even though Slocum could only see one man, he had been in enough dangerous situations to know that it was highly unlikely that he would be braced by a lone gunman. The man at the other end of the stable had been waiting for him, and Slocum would bet his bottom dollar that there was at least one more man somewhere close by who was ready to tip the odds in the loudmouth's favor.

Slocum was even more convinced that he was about to face another hidden gunman when he saw that the man he could see in front of him had not made a move to draw his pistol. Slocum waited, ready to slip his pistol from its holster and fire at anyone who moved in a threatening manner.

"I got him, Baker," a voice shouted, and Slocum saw the door of the tack room swing open.

A man emerged from the tack room, six-gun blazing orange flame. Slocum felt a bullet whistle past his ear, then thud into the wooden stable wall. A second shot boomed out as Slocum moved further to his right, drawing his pistol from its holster in one smooth motion. The bullet spanged into the wall right behind where he was. The shooter who had hidden in the tack room was good.

Baker drew his pistol, but Slocum was faster. He fired from the hip and saw his bullet catch Baker just above the belt buckle just as the man had his pistol half out of its holster.

Baker grunted, then screamed out in pain as his body slammed backward from the impact of the .45-caliber bullet and part of his spine came apart while his belly gushed blood.

Slocum dropped to his knees and swung his pistol on the other man who was just firing his third shot. Slocum fired a split second later, then flung himself headlong to the floor of the stable. He heard the bullet whine just over his head and the hairs on the back of his neck bristled like the hackles on a cat's back.

"Ahh," the shooter said as Slocum's bullet slammed into his side, throwing him into a twisting, off-balance jerk that knocked his legs out from under him. His fourth shot, reflexive at that point, sped harmlessly through the ceiling above his head as he landed flat on his back.

Slocum drew his feet under him and cocked the hammer of his Colt. He ran toward the two downed men, ready to shoot again if either made a move to fire his pistol.

He stood over the man who had hidden in the tack room. He was alive, but obviously in a great deal of pain.

"Well, what'll it be?" Slocum asked. "I've got one with your name written on it, ready to put between your eyes."

"Damn you, Slocum," the wounded man said, through clenched teeth.

"Drop the pistol," Slocum said, "or I'll air you out a little more."

Just then, Lucy came dashing into the stables. She stopped next to Slocum and looked down at the wounded man. She gasped and turned to Slocum. But before she could say anything, the wounded man swung his pistol toward Slocum. Lucy and Slocum heard the ominous *snap-click* as the man cocked the pistol. Before he could fire, Slocum shot him between the eyes at point-blank range. The bullet blew a small, dark hole in the man's forehead. The skin around it began to turn blue as the blood inside was sealed off by the force of the bullet. The back of his head blew apart like a pie plate and a pool of blood began to form in the dirt beneath his head. His eyes rolled into the back of their sockets and then settled back straight in a ghastly stare. He twitched once, then lay still, his pistol falling to his side, his dead finger still curled inside the trigger guard. Slocum gingerly pulled the pistol from his grasp, lest rigor mortis complete the trigger squeeze and claim a victim after the man's death.

"My God," Lucy exclaimed. "That's Harry Lawton you just killed."

"Couldn't be helped, Lucy. He was going to shoot both of us, if he could."

"You didn't have to kill him, did you? Couldn't you have just wounded him?"

"He was wounded. And he had a loaded pistol, already cocked."

"But do you know who you just killed?"

"You mentioned his name. Harry Lawton, wasn't it?"

"Yes. I wish you hadn't killed him. He was hurt. He might not have been able to shoot you. Or me."

"Sometimes, a split second means the difference between life and death," Slocum said. "This was one of those times. This man bushwhacked me. He hid himself in the tack room. He would have killed me, if he could have, and then he would have killed you."

"How do you know that?"

"Your name was mentioned a time or two. As 'that damned woman,' or some such."

Lucy shuddered as she looked down at the corpse of Harry Lawton.

"Harry Lawton," she said again. "I might have known he would be here."

"You suspected he might be here?" Slocum asked.

"I-I thought it was a possibility. I should have told you about him."

"There's a lot you didn't tell me, evidently," he said, a trace of dry sarcasm in his voice.

"Oh, John, I'm so sorry. So many things have been happening, and all so fast, I just didn't think."

"What else do I need to know, Lucy, before I ride into Belleville up in Holcomb Valley?"

"I'll tell you on the way, John. We must get away from here. No telling how many more men are trying to kill you."

Slocum walked over to the other man, Baker. Lucy followed. "Do you know this one?" he asked.

"Yes," she said, cringing at the sight of the wounded man. "His name's Ralph Baker. He works for Lawton. He's still alive, isn't he?"

Slocum looked down at Baker, who was holding his belly. His hand was covered with blood that had spurted out through the hole above his belt buckle. His eyes were closed tightly, as if he were in great pain. But Slocum knew that he had probably not felt pain right away. He had observed animals and men who had been shot, and the impact of the bullet seemed to put them in shock at first, so that some men didn't even know they had been shot. He had seen that in the war many times. He had come across badly wounded men who felt no pain and had talked to some who did not even know they were mortally wounded and did not have long to live.

There was a large pool of blood welling up in the dirt under Baker's back, more blood than a man could spare and still live.

"This man won't last out the day," Slocum said. "But he and Lawton called the turn. They opened the ball. It's too damned bad."

"Oh," she said and turned away, filled with fear and revulsion at what she had seen. "John, we'd better get out of here. And real fast. I'm sure people heard the shots and it will be a lot better for both of us if we're not here when someone comes to find out what the shooting was all about."

"You're right," he said. "Can you saddle up your own horse? I'll take care of Tad's horse and mine."

"Yes, of course. But hurry."

Slocum and Lucy finished saddling up their horses in just a few minutes. Lucy was nervous, but when she had finished cinching up her saddle, she was first to leave the stables. Slocum led Tad's claybank mare out a few seconds later.

"Point the way," he told Lucy.

"Follow me," she said, and put her horse, a bay mare she called Rosie, into a trot. The horses were frisky at first, but Slocum knew they had been grained and he had taken a few hatfuls for the trip, although he did not know how long the ride to Holcomb Valley would take them. He was now completely dependent on Lucy to show him the way.

Outside of Victor, Slocum caught up to Lucy and pulled up alongside. They had ridden up a gulley and then on a slant to climb up the sidehill until they were on flat terrain that seemed to stretch forever. From there, Lucy rode on a path through the brush that brought them to a well-rutted road that showed signs of having seen much wagon, horse and cattle traffic. The ground was well packed and, in places, showed signs of flash flooding from the frequent storms that blew through that part of the country. California, Slocum mused, was a land of many parts, beautiful, cruel, majestic at times, brutally harsh at others.

The land was thick with cactus, Joshua trees, yucca, sagebrush and scrub. In the distance he could see the bluish outline of the mountains, with the sun just poking up over the eastern horizon, a blazing ball of fire that threatened a hot day on the high desert.

The road followed a path parallel with the mountain range, and he saw signs where it had been hacked out of the desert by men who had made trails in the wilderness in the interest of commerce. But he saw no cattle ranches, no sign of human habitation as far as his eye could see.

"That's the San Bernardino range off to your right," Lucy said. "Later on, we're going to ride right up into them, up to Holcomb Valley."

"And the town up there is Belleville?"

"Yes. It almost became the county seat, but the politicians didn't want to live in the mountains or ride into them, so it's now in the town of San Bernardino."

"Founded by the good fathers, I take."

"Yes. The Spanish put up missions all over the country and San Bernardino was one of them."

"Who was Lawton?" Slocum asked suddenly, as if still trying to figure out why Lawton and Baker had not only jumped him, but had been determined to put his lamp out.

"You seemed pretty upset that I had to kill him."

"He was the cousin of the constable in Belleville, Sidney Lawton. And Sid is a very powerful man."

"And what about the Baker fellow? How does he fit in?"

"Baker happened to be Sid Lawton's favorite nephew. They were family, those two."

"Well, those boys were obviously both friends of Beddoes. I guess that means Beddoes and Lawton are good friends."

"I forgot to tell you that."

"Among other things," Slocum said sarcastically.

"Oh, you don't have to be mean about it, John. I've been in a state of confusion ever since you came to Victor."

"But you're not confused now," he said.

"No. The sun is coming up and the air tastes good. I don't even mind that I've had very little sleep."

"How long is the ride to Holcomb Valley?" he asked, looking over at the mountains, which were starting to bristle with pines now that the sun was shedding more light on them.

"Oh, we can't make it all the way today," she said.

"Are there any towns between here and there?"

"No, John. We're going to have to lay out our bedrolls and sleep under the stars. By the way, how are those wounds?"

"They hurt, and one of them is starting to itch."

"It must be healing then."

"I reckon." He looked all around and saw how empty the land was, and how full, at the same time. "Just where do you plan to do this sleeping under the stars?" he asked.

She pointed ahead and smiled.

"Partway up the steep grade to Holcomb Valley there's a little place we can stop and make camp."

"Steep grade?"

"Yes. We'd kill the horses if we tried to ride to Belleville in one day. Oh, it could be done and has been done, but I am thinking we don't want to get into Belleville all worn out."

"No," he said, "we wouldn't want that."

He wondered what he had gotten himself into by hooking up with Lucy Bancroft. Getting his mules back was one thing, but now it seemed there was a price on her head, as well as on his.

7

Slocum kept looking back down the road to see if they were being followed. But he saw no telltale dust, nor could he see anyone on their trail. Late in the afternoon, they passed a rock outcropping on the left, a landmark that he had been watching for some miles. He dug out a cheroot and lit it as he gazed at the high pile of rocks. Something about it caught his eye. A moment later, he spotted something off to the side of the road. He stopped, leaning down to look at it more closely.

"That looks like a cannonball," he said. "From a four-pounder, unless I miss my guess."

"I don't know what a four-pounder is, but it is a cannonball," Lucy said. "Did you see all those small ruts we passed?"

"Yes," he said. "All pointing toward that big pile of rocks over yonder."

"Where we turn off this road and head into the mountains," Lucy said, "there used to be an army fort. It's still there, but abandoned now. Those rocks there were where the Serrano Indians made their last stand."

"Last stand?" Slocum asked.

"According to all I've heard, the U.S. Army wiped out the entire tribe of Serranos. They set up their field pieces out here on the plain and besieged the last ones who were behind those rocks."

"I don't like to hear about such things," Slocum said. "But I know this is not the first place the Indians were driven from their homes, killed off."

"My father used to tell me that this was the price of civilization."

"And the Serranos paid the price," Slocum said.

"Yes, I guess so."

Slocum knew what it was like to be driven from home. After the war, he had come home to find that carpetbaggers had invaded the South, and what the Union army had started, many of these scurrilous men had finished. He could sympathize with the Serrano Indians. With his own eyes he had seen worse atrocities when he had ridden with Quantrill after General Price had assigned him to the madman.

When Slocum returned home after the war, he found that his mother and father were both dead and his farm had been seized by a carpetbagger for back taxes. That's when he learned that Georgia was under "reconstruction" and those in the government were as crooked and as vile as poisonous snakes.

Slocum lived with those bitter memories of the war and its aftermath in Calhoun County, Georgia, and seeing that place where the Serranos had been wiped out brought much of it boiling back up in his memory.

"A penny for your thoughts, John," Lucy said.

"They're not worth that much," he said. "Let's ride on."

The sun cleared the eastern horizon, the range of mountains that loomed above the high desert. The air was crisp and clear, the sky a soft blue, and there was a scent of wildflowers in the air as Lucy and Slocum rode on, following the wagon road to a pass that would take them into the high valley called Holcomb.

They stopped briefly beside the road where Lucy surprised Slocum with the fare she had brought, slabs of ham lathered with mustard between slices of thick sourdough bread, dried apples and even a savory cheese. Slocum resisted the impulse to wolf the food down as they sat in the shade of a Joshua tree that, from a distance, resembled a man lifting his arms in supplication.

"I'll bet you even have supper in those saddlebags of yours," Slocum said.

"I'll bet I do, too."

"And you even filled my canteen. You were pretty busy last night. Did you get any sleep at all?"

"Not much," she said.

"This trip is pretty important to you, isn't it?"

"I want the man who ordered my father's death brought to justice," she said. "And I want to see the men who killed him brought to trial and sentenced for their crimes."

"There is very little justice in this world," Slocum said.

"I believe there is justice in the world, John. It's just that it's not always swift."

"Very seldom swift," Slocum said.

"I know you were in the war, and you probably saw a lot of terrible things, including injustice," Lucy said.

"I saw a lot, all right," Slocum said. "And not all in the war."

"I'd like to hear about it sometime, John. Your experiences, I mean."

"They would make for pretty dull listening, I'm thinking."

"Oh, I doubt it." She chewed her sandwich slowly, taking dainty bites. She had even set out a serviette that they both shared. She wiped the corners of her mouth with one end of the napkin, leaving Slocum the majority of the unsoiled portion. His stomach roiled with the first swallow of food, then settled down as he ate and washed down the ham and bread with trickles of water from the canteen.

When they were finished, Lucy folded the white serviette and tucked it back into her saddlebag. "Did you get enough food?" she asked.

"I don't like to each much in heat like this, or when I'm riding a ways."

"Neither do I. I just didn't want you to starve to death. And, you have lost some blood. Perhaps I should check your wounds again before we go on."

"There's no need. I'm not bleeding and I'm not hurting. Let's ride on."

He stood up and looked back down the road. This time he saw twin spools of dust along the road and, behind them, a thin haze of sand hanging in the air.

"Two riders, I figure," he said. "Coming pretty fast. Too fast in this heat."

The sun had risen almost to its zenith and he was beginning to sweat. The riders were too far away to tell who they might be. But they were coming from Victor at a fast gallop.

Lucy followed Slocum's gaze and shaded her eyes from the sun.

"Know who they are?" Slocum asked as the two riders drew closer.

"No. They're too far away."

"Those horses will founder at that pace. Are there any ranches around, or stage stops where they might change horses?"

"There's no stage stop, but sometimes there are horses at the old army post at the foot of the grade that takes us up to the pass. I think the stage line keeps spare horses there in case any horses are hurt between Belleville and the valley, or between Victor and the army post."

"Oh?" he said. "They run a stage line along here?"

"The Barstow stage travels between Barstow and Holcomb Valley. In fact, it's due along here pretty soon."

Slocum looked up at the sky and marked the location of the sun. It was not yet noon. He didn't know how far it was to Holcomb Valley, but he would bet hard coin that whoever was riding their way meant to make it up into the mountains before nightfall.

"Could those riders, if they changed horses at the fort, make it to Holcomb Valley today?" he asked.

"Yes. That's more than halfway, in miles. They'd ride in after dark, but they could make it."

"It looks to me as if that's what they're aiming to do," Slocum said, his eyes staying on the riders who were still churning up dust.

"I don't think they can see us," Lucy said.

"We'll stay low, but see if you recognize either of them."

"I will," Lucy said. She stood on her tiptoes to see

through the blooming yucca and the Joshua trees. Slocum studied each man as they drew closer, the way they sat their horses, what they were wearing. He committed what he saw to memory in case he ran into either man again.

"Recognize either of them?" Slocum asked as the riders reached their nearest point to them.

"That one man, with the Mexican sombrero. He's a friend of Harry and Sid Lawton's. He's a—I think you call them gunslingers, one of those. His name is Little Bill Jones. Or that's what they call him."

"And the other man?" Slocum asked.

"Just a minute. I'm still trying to . . ." Her voice trailed away and her mouth dropped open as recognition struck her. "My God," Lucy exclaimed.

"What?" Slocum asked.

"I-I can't believe it. I thought she left Belleville for good. After my father died. I always thought she had something to do with his death, but I never could figure out what. But she's mixed up in it anyway."

"Who? Are you telling me that's a woman riding with Little Bill?"

Lucy turned to Slocum and looked him straight in the eye, her lips quivering with rage, her eyes wide, flaring with anger.

"Unless I'm mistaken," she said, "that's a woman riding with Little Bill, and her name is Alexis Contreras. She was thick with Luke Chadwick, and after my mother died, she made a play for my father. But he never trusted her."

Slocum looked more closely at the other rider. He could see now that Lucy was right, the other rider was a woman. But she rode her horse like a man, straight-backed, easy in the saddle. She wore men's clothing, too: pants, shirt, a flat-crowned hat that was gray. He barely caught a glimpse of her ample breasts as she passed by, which was the only way he could tell that she was a woman.

"She doesn't look like a Mexican," Slocum said. "Her hair is piled up under her hat, but her complexion is fair."

"She's not a Mexican," Lucy said. "She's Swedish, or German, I think. But, she married a wealthy Mexican by the name of Pedro Contreras, who died mysteriously."

"Mysteriously?"

"Some said he was poisoned. But this was never proven. Pedro owned a huge rancho in San Bernardino and property in Big Bear Lake, which is in a valley below Holcomb. Alexis now owns it all."

"I see," Slocum said. "Well, that's quite a pair we saw riding by, then. A gunslinger and a widow."

"Alexis can ride and shoot as well as any man. I've seen her do it. She raises fine Arabian horses and that's one of them she's riding now."

"Yes, I noticed that. Fine horseflesh."

"I wonder what she was doing in Victor," Lucy mused. "And with Little Bill Jones. I didn't even think they knew each other."

"They know each other, all right," Slocum said. "And my bet is that they're riding hell-bent-for-leather to warn Beddoes and Deakins that we're coming their way."

"And, don't forget Luke Chadwick, the man I believe is responsible for killing my father."

"Belleville, and Holcomb Valley, is beginning to look more and more like a den of thieves."

"Oh, there are good people there. Most of them are good. But there are a few evil men."

"And women, apparently."

"Yes, and women," Lucy said.

When the riders had passed from view, Slocum indicated that Lucy should mount up. "We can't catch them, you know," she said.

"I know. Let them tell their tales up in Holcomb Valley. That way, when we get there tomorrow, we won't have to wait so long for Beddoes, Deakins and their boss, Chadwick, to show their hands."

"Do you have a plan, then?" Lucy asked.

"No, not really," Slocum said, as he swung into the saddle. "Sometimes it's best not to make plans."

"Why?"

"Plans can go wrong. I prefer to watch which way people jump."

"But they can jump someplace you least expect, John."

"Oh, I didn't say I wouldn't prepare. If you think a thing through, figure out every way a person can jump, then you'll be ready. In fact, if a man thinks hard enough, he'll know where a man's going to jump even before he does."

"I don't think I follow you," she said.

"It's not important. Beddoes and Deakins have already dealt the cards. All I can do is sit down at their table and play my own hand."

"I'm worried that something might happen to you," she said.

"Well, the good thing about a card game is that most of the cards are hidden from the other players. In this case, however, Chadwick has already shown most of his hand. Besides Beddoes and Deakins, there's Little Bill and Alexis."

"And don't forget Sid Lawton."

"I'm not. He's the wild card. But what I thought was going to be a game of five-card draw is looking more and more like seven-card stud."

"Poker. To you, it's a poker game."

Slocum smiled.

"Yes, and this one tells me the joker is wild."

8

The dust raised by the two riders had barely settled back to earth by the time Lucy and Slocum got back to the stage road. But Slocum could still taste the particles of sand that clung to his teeth and could still smell the faint aroma that clung to the air.

The road began to curve toward the mountains, angling ever eastward through the tall yucca and the Joshua trees. Somewhere, in the distance, a quail piped its plaintive song, one of the lookouts perched atop the tallest yucca, where it could see for miles in every direction in the crystal-clear air.

"I notice we're heading toward the mountains now," Slocum said.

"Yes," Lucy replied. "But they're farther away than they look."

"I know," Slocum said.

"You can't see the pass from here unless you know where it is."

"I'd say we're less than ten miles from it, though."

"You read the distance pretty good," she said.

Slocum said nothing. He was still pondering all that had happened since he and Tad rode into Victor. He missed the kid, was sorry that he'd never see his kin in San Bernardino, never live to play with his grandchildren. Like so many boys he had known in the war, killed before their time, if one chose to look at life that way. The Indians of the Plains, he knew, believed that once they reached the age of twelve, their lives were complete and full. Which was why, perhaps, they were so brave in battle and were not afraid to die.

But the boys his age he had known in the war were all afraid to die, and each one that lived beyond that first shock of a lead ball hitting their vitals, called out for their mothers. And for many, those were their last words.

"Do you know if Tad had any family?" Slocum asked suddenly.

"Not that I know of," she said.

He hadn't known much about Tad. Perhaps he had been an orphan. Some of the boys who had died at Gettysburg had been orphans, and there were times when he had wished he'd had no parents to grieve for because the grieving was hard. When his father died and he knew he'd never see him again, he felt as if William Slocum had left a big hole where he had once been. It was the same with his brother, and when his mother had died, he had felt like an orphan. He had felt as if someone had come along and cut his legs out from under him, and it took him a long time to regain his feet and climb out of that black hole of grief and get back to living.

"Why do you ask, John?" Lucy looked over at him as she rode alongside.

"I was just curious. I wish someone from his family could have been with Tad when he died."

"Yes, that would have been nice. He looked so small and sad on that bed. So alone."

"We're each of us alone when we die, I think. At that last moment."

"I don't like to think of such things," Lucy said.

"When we're young, death is way off in the distance. It's something that happens to other people."

"I know what you mean," she said. "I never really knew what death was until my mother died. I still thought it was some kind of mistake. But when I saw death up close, what they did to my father, I think that's when the full force of death really sank in. I know now that death is just a breath away at all times."

"That's valuable knowledge," Slocum said. "It might keep you alive."

"What do you mean?"

"Now that you know what death is, and how sudden it can happen, you'll keep your eyes and ears open and be looking for it. Then you have a chance to let it pass by."

"Is that what you were thinking back there in Victor when you shot those two men this morning?"

"I wasn't thinking of anything but protecting myself. And you."

"But you knew you might be killed."

"Yes, there's always that chance. If a man comes gunning for you, that is not the time to hope something or someone will come along to save you."

"Don't you feel badly, though, about taking a life?"

"I value life, the same as any man, or woman. But when you're looking death in the face, the minute you start checking with your conscience, you're dead."

"But you have a conscience, don't you? Doesn't everyone?"

"I think I do," Slocum said. "I've known men who had none. They could kill as easily as you and I can breathe. There's something missing in some people, and I think that's why we have killers who put no value whatsoever on human life. Or any kind of life."

"But you do," she said, a slight tremor in her voice.

"Yes, I care about life and I plan to live it a long time."

Lucy sighed, as if relieved by Slocum's answer. "I'm glad," she said. Then a moment later, she exclaimed: "Uh-oh."

"What is it?" Slocum asked.

"There comes the Barstow stage." She looked up at the sun, which was falling toward the western horizon. "And right on time, or pretty near," she added.

"It looks to be about fifteen or twenty minutes from us, if it keeps at its present speed. Do we want them to see us?" Slocum asked.

"No," Lucy said quickly. "We've got to get off the road."

"Why?"

"There's no telling who might be on that stage," she said. "Besides, I'm almost certain that Alexis and Little Bill gave the driver and all his passengers an earful about what happened in Victor over the last two days."

"I think you may be right," Slocum said. "Let's ride off into the brush and get out of sight if we can."

"Yes," Lucy said tightly, and Slocum wondered once again how much more she wasn't telling him about herself and the men he was chasing.

Lucy led the way, and Slocum followed as she rode into a little draw and dismounted. He slid down off his horse and looked at the rim of the depression and saw that they could not be seen by anyone inside the coach, and probably not by the driver and whoever was riding shotgun. From where they were, he could not see the stage at all, but he knew it was coming. He kept both his horse and Tad's reined up tight and soothed them to silence as they waited for the stage to pass.

Slocum fished a cheroot out of his pocket, struck a lucifer and pulled the smoke into his mouth and lungs. When he blew it out, he waved a hand in front of his mouth to break up the smoke just in case one of the people on the stage had very sharp eyesight. He glanced over at Lucy, who was crouched down, even though she was shorter than her horse's shoulder. She was trembling slightly, but tried to conceal her nervousness.

"What's the matter?" Slocum asked. "Nobody on that stage can see you."

"I'm not taking any chances," she said, more quickly than Slocum thought seemed necessary.

"Why? Do you know the stage driver? Or someone on that particular stage run?"

"No—I don't know. They have several drivers. I don't know who's on the stage."

"Then why are you so nervous?" Slocum asked.

"I-I'm not nervous. I just don't want any trouble before we get to Holcomb Valley."

Slocum drew deeply on his cheroot and let the smoke seep slowly from his mouth. Lucy was still shaking and she turned away from him so that he couldn't look into her eyes.

"Even if the people on the stage know about me," he said, "there's not much they can do out here. I'm sure the passengers want to get to Victor or Barstow, and the driver must have a schedule to keep."

"I don't know," she snapped. "Just stop asking all these questions, will you, please?"

"I intend to keep asking them until I get some straight answers from you," Slocum said, striding toward her. She turned her back on him and he grasped her shoulders and spun her around so that she could not escape his scathing gaze. "Now, just what is the real reason you don't want anyone on that stage to see us?"

Lucy dropped her head, as if in shame. Slocum put a hand under her chin and tilted her head back up so that he could look into her eyes. What he saw then made him wonder about her even more. Her eyes were wet and he saw that she was beginning to spill tears.

"All right," he said, "just calm down. Something's bothering you real bad right now, and if you don't want to tell me, I won't force you. But if we're in this together, and you want my help, you'll damn sure stop keeping secrets from me."

"Oh, John," she whispered. "What have I gotten you into?"

"I don't know. But you didn't do it all by yourself, Lucy. I'm the man who brought the mules to Victor and it was my friend Tad who was killed. So, I'm in it, like it or not. But if your interests bump up against mine and stop me from doing what I have to do, guess which way I'll go on this."

"Damn you. Why do you have to be so smart?"

Slocum ignored the question. He knew it didn't require an answer. He continued to hold her head up and look into Lucy's eyes, waiting for her to tell him what she couldn't seem to say to his face.

"Be-before I left Belleville," she stammered, "I overheard some men talking at the bar in the Octagon House. That's the hotel in Belleville where most of the town gathers to gossip and talk business."

"And what did you overhear?" Slocum asked.

"These were men who worked for Luke Chadwick and as soon as I got close, they shut up. But I heard enough to make me angry."

"Go on," Slocum said.

"They were talking about a shipment of gold going out on the Barstow stage in four days. They said it was gold that had come from my father's mine. I heard them say the name of the mine, even though Chadwick has changed it since he stole it from my father."

"All right. So, they're shipping gold out on the stage. Are you mad because it's stolen gold?"

"Well, yes, I am, of course, but I was curious, too."

"Why?"

"Because why would they ship gold to Barstow when the assayer's office is in San Bernardino, and if they were selling the gold, wouldn't it go from San Bernardino to Los Angeles and then up to San Francisco to the mint?"

"I don't know that much about gold," Slocum said.

"Well, I know my father and everyone else who mined gold in Holcomb Valley sent the raw ore down to San Bernardino to be assayed and then to a refinery in Los Angeles. And if they were selling the gold to the government, it always went by ship to San Francisco."

"Okay. So, maybe Chadwick wants the gold to go to Barstow to be assayed. I saw an assay office there when we passed through."

"At first, I thought these men were talking about the gold going to Barstow, but, later, I realized that I had jumped to the wrong conclusion."

"What do you mean?" Slocum asked.

"Well, these men were sitting at the end of the bar and I was in a corner talking to a friend of mine, a barmaid who works there. I distinctly heard one of the men say, 'The gold will be on the Barstow stage.' And then the other man laughed and said something I couldn't quite hear all of. But later I realized I had heard this man say, 'Too bad it ain't goin' to Barstow like everybody thinks.' "

"I wonder what he meant by that?"

Lucy shook her head. "I have no idea. But that's what I heard. And I wondered, why would they want people to think the gold was going to Barstow on the stage?"

"Maybe they're taking it to Victor."

"I thought of that. They could take the gold to Victor and then go through Cajon Pass to San Bernardino. It's the long way around, but sometimes the roads down the mountain are closed and that's the way people go from Holcomb Valley to San Bernardino."

Slocum saw that Lucy was still shaking. He released her chin and she dried her eyes.

"There was something else you heard, too, wasn't there?" he asked.

Lucy started to shake her head, then thought better of it. He saw that she was wrestling with herself, perhaps wondering if she should tell him the rest of it.

"Before these men shut up, after they saw me in the corner with my friend, Betsy Carmichael, I heard one of them say, 'Chadwick says that if we see that Bancroft woman, we put her lamps out.' "

"And you took that to mean . . ." Slocum said.

"That they were to kill me," Lucy said.

Again, Slocum felt a cold chill crawl up his spine and the hairs on the back of his neck began to tingle as if they had been charged by static electricity.

9

Slocum heard the stage pass by on the road a few hundred yards away. He took another long puff on his cheroot and let the smoke warm his throat and lungs before he blew it out. He licked his dry lips and then drew Lucy to him, putting his arm around her. He gave her a squeeze to calm her down, then let out a long sigh.

"Did those men in the saloon think you were going to try and stop the stage?" he asked. "Or, did they know you were going to Victor?"

"I had heard that you were bringing some mules to Victor and I told some people up there that I was going down to meet you."

"Why did you ride down to meet me?"

"I know," she said. "I've kept you in the dark about a lot of things, but I rode down to warn you."

"You knew that Beddoes and Deakins were going to steal my mules from me?"

"They were laughing and joking about it for weeks. Betsy overheard Beddoes and Deakins talking about it at

Octagon House. They didn't think anyone was listening, I guess."

"Did you find out why they asked for my services?" Slocum asked.

"Apparently, they knew who you were. And, I gathered that one of Chadwick's men or someone in his outfit had a grudge against you."

"Do you know who that was, Lucy?"

"No. They never mentioned a name. Just said that it would be payback time when they got you in their gun sights."

"Well, that's another worry, I guess. I've made some enemies in my life."

"I'm sure you have, John."

Slocum finished smoking his cheroot. He ground the stub out under his boot heel and let the reins out that were holding Sugar as he made to mount the Palouse.

"Are we going on, then?" Lucy asked.

"Yes," Slocum said. "It is payback time, as they said."

Lucy climbed into the saddle without any help from Slocum and as he watched her climb up, he felt a tug of desire for her. She was wearing a long dress that didn't hide her figure. And as he put his boot into his stirrup, he thought of how it had been the night before. Even in the blazing sun, he thought, he wanted her again.

The road was empty when Slocum and Lucy regained it and headed toward the mountains. The road kept cutting back until it was straight, but he was surprised to see a fork in the road a half hour later.

"We keep going straight," Lucy said. "That fork leads to Old Woman Springs and more desert beyond. It's mostly used by prospectors and brigands."

"Brigands?"

"Thieves, robbers. Oh, yes, the law is scarce out here. There are a lot of places to hide in the high desert."

"And in the mountains, too," Slocum said.

"Yes, of course. Dead Horse Canyon lies yonder," she said, pointing to a far niche in the foothills to their left. "The constable and a posse chased a robber there once, so the story goes, and found his dead horse. He walked out of the mountains and escaped into the desert."

"Every place I've ever been has its share of stories and legends," Slocum said.

"And this part of California is no different," Lucy said, kicking her heels into the flanks of her horse. "We'd better hurry if we're going to get to our camping place before it gets dark."

Slocum followed her as he mulled over all that she had told him when they were hiding back there in the draw. He also was looking at the road, reading tracks out of habit. Sometimes a man could tell a lot by what he saw on the ground, for men always left some sign of their presence. He saw nothing unusual however, and when, an hour or so later, he looked up, the mountains were very near. He could see the tall pines on the ridges and the smaller trees, scrub juniper and pinyon, clinging to the slopes.

Then Slocum saw the very tops of buildings off to the right of what looked like a canyon entrance to the mountains. He saw the thin traces of the road they were on rising upward until it disappeared from view where the canyon walls seemed to fold in on it.

"That's the old fort just ahead," Lucy said, pointing.

"I see the rooftops."

"A half hour's ride from here."

She slowed her horse and Slocum caught up and rode beside her, his senses now fully alert. He checked the Colt and loosened it in his holster. There was no telling what they might find up ahead, but he was pretty sure they'd find two horses that had been "rode hard and put away wet," as the saying went.

Slocum took the lead, waving a hand to signal Lucy that she should stay behind him. He approached the buildings cautiously and saw that what she had called a fort was not a fort at all, but more of an outpost. It was definitely military, or had been, but there were no fortifications that he could see, no gun or cannon ports, just a long line of low buildings, some of which appeared to have been stables. And there were the broken-down remains of corrals, all three-sided, using the rock of the mountain as a natural back wall.

It was very quiet as Slocum rode up, his eyes squinted to pick up any sudden movement. As he approached, he heard a horse whinny, and then another. The Palouse pricked its ears and cocked them forward for a moment before beginning to twist in order to locate the direction where the horses might be.

Slocum reined up short and reached for the butt of his pistol as he saw a man step out of the shadowed doorway of the main building. Lucy stopped just behind him.

"Recognize him?" Slocum asked.

"No, I don't," she said.

"He looks to be an old man."

"Yes. An old man who needs a shave."

The man had a long gray beard, and his hair was long, too. He was hatless, but as Slocum looked closer, he saw that the man held a battered felt hat in one hand. He thought, at first, that the hat could be shielding a weapon, but the man stepped out into the sunlight and put the hat on top of his head. He appeared to be unarmed.

"Well, you all can come in," the man said. "I don't bite. Leastwise, I ain't bit nobody lately."

Slocum studied the man as he rode in. He decided that the man's smile was false. He was hiding something, trying to put them at ease. Before Slocum dismounted, he glanced up at the pass and the surrounding folds of mountain. Such a place could conceal many things, including a man with a rifle, or a woman.

"Light down. Ain't got much to offer. Water and feed for your horses, some shade."

Slocum wrapped the reins of both horses around a hitch rail as Lucy stepped from her saddle. There was no shade out in front of the buildings. The sun was falling away to the west, still boiling in the afternoon sky.

"Name's Barney," the old man said, extending his hand to Slocum.

"I'm Slocum."

"Pleased to meetcha," Barney said.

"You keep horses here?"

"Sometimes, yep."

"Two people passed by here. A man and a woman. Did they change horses?"

"Well, sir, you sure ask a lot of questions right off."

"And are you going to answer them?"

"I reckon. Not that it's any of your business, Slocum."

"I'd like to look around, if you don't mind."

"Well, now, I don't own this place, so you go ahead. Ain't much to see, though."

Lucy tied up her horse and walked over. Barney stared at her for a minute. Slocum thought he saw a flash of recognition in Barney's eyes, which quickly disappeared. Lucy put out her hand and introduced herself. Barney gave her the same stock greeting he had given Slocum.

Slocum didn't wait for permission, but slid his rifle out of its boot and started walking to the end of the building.

"Where you goin' with that rifle?" Barney asked.

"I want to see the stock you have here," Slocum said. "What horses you have boarded."

"You ain't a-goin' to shoot them, are you?"

"No. But if someone takes a potshot at me from those hills, I want to be able to return fire."

Slocum reached the end of the building and started to walk toward the back.

"What makes you think somebody's going to take a shot at you?" Barney asked.

"That seems to be what people in these parts have on their minds."

"Well, damn," Barney muttered, and Slocum disappeared around the end of the building. He saw the corrals and several horses in one, some in another. The corrals adjoined the buildings farther down and he smelled the manure that had accumulated. There was a door open at one corral where he saw the two horses ridden by Alexis and Little Bill.

When he walked up on them, he saw that they had been dried and curried. Their coats gleamed in the sun and their mains glistened as they shook their heads when he approached. He looked at all the brands, but did not recognize any of them. He noted their designs, though, in case he saw other such brands up in Holcomb Valley.

The door led to a stable, which was dark inside. But no one took a shot at him, and Slocum walked around the building and back out front where Lucy and Barney were standing, talking to each other.

"Find what you were lookin' for?" Barney asked.

"I see the Arabian and the chestnut gelding," Slocum said.

"Yep, I done grained and curried 'em."

"Are you here all the time?" Slocum asked.

"Nope. I come and go whenever I'm told."

"And who do you work for?"

"Well, sir, I work odd jobs for a lot of people," Barney said.

"So, who paid you to come down and keep fresh horses here?"

"Well, the Belleville to Barstow stage line for one."

"And who paid you to have fresh horses for Alexis and Little Bill?" Slocum asked.

"Well, now, Slocum, that just may not be none of your business."

Slocum swung the barrel of the rifle up to bear on Barney's belly and held it steady.

"You ain't jacked no shell into the chamber of that Henry, have you?" Barney asked.

"I might have. Want to find out for sure? And, it's a Winchester, Barney, a '73."

Barney's face turned ashen as he stared at the muzzle of the Winchester. Beads of sweat began to form along the top crease line in his forehead. Lucy took two steps backward, leaving Barney standing alone.

A silence built up between the three people. Lucy stood stock-still, watching both Slocum and Barney as if hypnotized. Slocum held the rifle steady on Barney's gut. Barney tried to swallow, but when he opened his mouth to gulp air, the muscles in his neck quivered as if something was stuck in his throat.

Finally, Barney found his voice. His words came out in a throaty croak. "All right, Slocum, I ain't goin' to call your bluff. Mr. Chadwick told me to bring fresh horses down, that whole remuda back there, and just wait."

"Did he tell you why?"

"He said someone might come by and need 'em."

"And did someone come by and need those horses?"

"Well, first there was two men a-drivin' a string of mules. They switched mounts. And today, there was that Alexis woman and, as you said, Little Bill. They both come by a-needin' fresh horses."

"And do you expect anybody else?"

"No, I reckon not. Not right away."

"So, what are you supposed to do?" Slocum asked. "Just keep waiting here and taking care of those horses back there?"

Barney hesitated. And then he did something that made Slocum want to drop him right where he stood. Barney turned slightly and looked up toward the mountains. Not at the pass, but at an outcropping of rocks that jutted out from the nearest foothill.

When Slocum followed the line of Barney's stare, he saw a flash of sunlight, a bright silver burst of light that was like a signaling mirror. But he knew it was no such thing.

Slocum took a step backward, lifted his rifle and pushed on the lever at the same time, jacking a shell into the chamber. Barney winced as he heard the mechanism click and the cartridge leave the magazine and slide into the breech of the rifle barrel.

"Duck!" Slocum shouted to Lucy a split second before he heard the crack of a rifle and the whine of a bullet speeding straight toward him.

10

Slocum cracked off a shot as he leaped sideways out of the line of fire. He heard the bullet buzz past him like an angry hornet as his Winchester recoiled. Out of the corner of his eye, he saw Lucy dive for the ground, and Barney went to his knees before falling face forward to hug the ground.

Slocum pressed himself against the wall of the building and levered another cartridge into the chamber as his gaze sought out the shooter in the rocks. A puff of white smoke lingered for a moment then wafted away and turned to filmy cobwebs on the slight afternoon breeze.

"Oooh," Lucy exclaimed and began to crawl for cover next to the building. Then there was another shot and a bullet plowed a furrow right next to Lucy's feet. She scrambled for the protection of the building's wall as Barney covered his head with both hands.

Slocum took aim at a spot just below where he saw the last puff of smoke and squeezed the trigger. The rifle bucked against his shoulder in recoil and he quickly levered another shell into the chamber. He saw a hat move and fired at it, holding low. He saw the hat take flight and sail off before it slammed into the rocks behind it and slid out of sight.

Slocum worked the lever again and hugged the wall of the building. His eyes narrowed to dark slits as he scanned the mountainside, looking for any movement, no matter how slight. A second or two later, he saw the glint of sun from a gun barrel that poked through the rocks. The shooter fired, but his aim was poor, and the shot went wild. Slocum took aim on the slit in the rocks and fired, hoping his bullet would fly true and find a target. He heard the whine of the ricochet and knew his aim had been a half-inch off, at least. He cursed under his breath and rammed another bullet into the breech.

It grew very quiet for several seconds. Slocum saw no movement in the rocks, but he knew his man was still up there. He also knew something else and that gave him some comfort. There was only one shooter up there, and that helped to even the odds.

Slocum began to edge along the wall. As he passed a cloudy, dust-covered window, he looked inside and saw bunk beds, indicating that this was an old army barracks that served the outpost. He kept his gaze locked on the rocks to the south, knowing that the closer he got to the shooter, the more he exposed himself.

He was surprised when he saw the snout of a rifle poke over a rock a few feet from where he had last seen the ambusher. He flattened himself against the barracks and waited.

Slocum did not have long to wait. A few seconds later, the rifle barked and he heard the sizzle of the bullet just before it ripped into the wall near his head, splintering off a chunk of weathered wood.

"Be careful," Lucy said, looking up at him from her prone position.

"See if you can get inside that barracks," Slocum told her. "You'll be safer there."

"All right," she said, and started to crawl toward the door, which was just beyond where Barney lay.

Slocum fired a quick shot, then started running toward the rocks, working the lever to slide another cartridge into the firing chamber. He stayed low and ran a zigzag pattern. The man in the rocks acted the way Slocum had expected him to. He stood up to get a better downward shot, exposing his head and upper torso.

The rifleman fired once, missed, kicking up a plume of dirt two yards to Slocum's right. Slocum fired back on the run, but managed to hold his rifle tightly against his shoulder and hold on the target. He squeezed the trigger, then ran straight for a closed door at the end of the far building where the stables were.

"You got him," Lucy yelled behind Slocum, but he couldn't see as he fought with the latch to open the door. He was very close to the rocks now and if there happened to be more than one shooter, he would be an easy target.

He heard a cry from the rocks, but it was short and muffled. He thought he heard a man curse, but he couldn't be sure. Perhaps Lucy was right. Maybe he had hit the bushwhacker with that running shot.

The latch lifted and the door opened. Slocum slipped inside, panting for breath. Hurriedly, he began to shove .44s into the magazine of the Winchester, wondering if he had kept an accurate count of the shots he had made.

When the magazine was full, he jacked another shell into the chamber and looked around him.

The stables were old, musty, and it was dark inside. There were small, high windows at the far end that were grimed over from age and weather, but some light leaked through. Slocum decided against trying to look out of them to see if he could spot the shooter. Instead, he walked to the opposite side of the stables and found another door. He slipped the latch and stepped outside before his eyes had become too accustomed to the darkness. Still, the sun was glaring and for a moment he could not see well.

He was shielded from the shooter for a few yards on that side of the building. He saw the horses milling in the corrals, but none gave away his presence. Slocum thought the gunfire might have spooked them some, but they were not kicking at the poles to get out.

Slocum reached the end of the building. He ducked low and peered around the corner, looking up into the jumble of rocks that the shooter had used for cover. He heard low groaning sounds, but at first, he could not see where they were coming from. He drew in a deep breath, held it and started running, hunched over, toward the base of the rock outcropping. Nobody shot at him and he reached a place of safety and concealment before he let out his breath.

Slocum waited and listened intently. That's when he heard a clatter of small stones. He bent his head back and looked upward. A small cascade of rocks began to tumble down like a miniature landslide. He moved to his right for a better look, and that's when he saw part of a man, a leg and an arm, through an opening in the boulders above him.

The man above Slocum was struggling with something. Slocum heard the sound of ripping cloth and then the man's sleeve came off his left arm. Slocum knew he was trying to make a tourniquet to stop the flow of blood. So, he figured, the man was wounded, but not seriously. At least not mortally, if he could stop the flow of blood.

Throwing caution to the wind, Slocum scrambled up the slope on a slant that took him away from the shooter, but afforded him protection among the rocks and boulders that jutted out from the hill. He kept his rifle ready and was prepared to finish the job if the shooter made any move to point a rifle in his direction.

"Who-who's there?" the man called as Slocum's boots knocked small pebbles and stones loose that rattled down the path he took.

Slocum said nothing, but gained ground and stood, finally, above the man who had been shooting his rifle at him.

The man's right sleeve had been ripped off, too, and his arm was bathed in blood. The bullet, Slocum figured, had caught him high in the shoulder or in the thick part of his upper arm. He was trying to tie the other sleeve above the wound to stop the flow of blood. His rifle lay wedged between two rocks. But he still had a pistol on his belt and one good arm.

"Just hold it steady," Slocum said. "One twitch, and I'll blow your head off."

The man turned around and looked up at the man in the black frock coat. His face was ashen and he grimaced in pain.

"Don't shoot, Slocum. You got me. I'm bad hurt."

"Step away from that rifle," Slocum ordered, "and drop that gun belt."

"I'll do 'er," the man said.

Slocum had never seen him before. He had a three-day beard, long, shaggy brown hair and a moustache that hadn't been trimmed in some time. His clothes were shabby and worn, heavy with dust and dirt, probably from lying in ambush among the rocks.

"Who in hell are you?" Slocum asked when the man stepped away from the rifle and, with his left hand, began to unbuckle his gun belt.

"Name's Don Williams."

"Who put you up to this?" Slocum asked, as the gun belt, with its holster and pistol, slid down the shooter's hips and fell to the ground. The pistol fell out and Slocum saw that it was a converted Remington .44 New Model Army that had once been percussion, but now fired regular .44-40 cartridges.

"If I tell you that, I'm as good as dead," Williams said.

"You'll die a lot quicker if you don't tell me," Slocum said.

Williams hesitated as if weighing his chances. He licked dry lips and held his right arm tightly to staunch the bleeding.

"I reckon I don't have much choice," Williams said.

"You don't have any choice, Williams. None at all."

"Well, it was Sid Lawton who hired me."

"To kill me?"

"No, to kill that Bancroft woman down there."

"Lucy Bancroft?"

"That's the one."

"Did Lawton send you after her?"

"Well, he said to wait here and if she came back from Victor to put her down. Permanent."

"Well, I was wondering if I had to take you up to Belleville and file charges against you with the constable," Slocum said. "But if Lawton hired you, I guess he probably wouldn't arrest you, would he?"

"I reckon if you took me up to Sid, he'd see to it that I never got out of his jail alive."

"Why would you work for a man like that? You don't trust him."

"No, well, I didn't apply for the job. Sid, he picked me, and said he'd drop all charges against me and I'd not have to pay no fines or nothin'."

"So, you were in jail up in Belleville?"

"Yeah, I was. For stealing, they said."

"Well, I'll tell you what, Williams. I'm going to set you free. Walk down there and apologize to Lucy Bancroft and I'll forget that you tried to shoot us. Do you have a horse in the corral?"

"No, I got off the stage when it come by."

"Then either you will have to bargain with Barney or walk to Victor."

"I don't know Barney."

"He's the man lying down there shaking like a dog shitting peach seeds."

Williams didn't laugh. Slocum gestured with his Winchester and Williams started to make his way down the hillside. Slocum stooped to pick up his rifle and gun belt, putting the Remington back in its holster. By the time he and Williams got to the barracks, Barney and Lucy were on their feet, waiting to find out what had happened.

"Do you know this man, Barney?" Slocum asked.

"Never saw him before in my life," Barney replied.

"I've seen him in Belleville," Lucy said. "He's a thief."

"I know," Slocum said. "I'm going to let him finish fixing his arm, then let him go his own way, as long as it's not back to Belleville. You got that, Williams?"

"I won't give you no more trouble," Williams said.

"That's right," Slocum said. "Barney, you're lucky I'm not sending you somewhere, too."

"What did I do?" Barney asked.

Slocum smiled. "I think you just might be in the wrong place at the wrong time, Barney. Here, take these." He handed Williams's rifle and gun belt over to Barney.

"Let's ride out of here, Lucy," Slocum said.

"Yes, we'd better go," she said, appearing slightly dazed by all that happened that day.

In moments, Slocum and Lucy were riding up through the pass as the sun continued to fall away in the west, throwing long shadows across the land.

"We'll just barely make our overnight stop before the sun goes down," Lucy said as the grade steepened.

"You know where we're going to stay tonight?"

"Yes. It's a place called . . . well, I'll keep that as a surprise," she said.

"You're full of surprises, Lucy."

"I think you are, too, John. That man back there. That thief. He wasn't trying to kill you, was he?"

"Oh, he was trying to put me out of action, all right."

"But he wasn't sent there to shoot you, am I right?"

"I'll keep that to myself for a time, too," Slocum said.

"See," she said. "You are a man full of secrets."

"A few, Lucy. A few."

They rode on, climbing ever higher into the San Bernardino Mountains.

11

The dusk came on suddenly, plunging the road into shadow, blurring all the landmarks, blotting out the sky as if someone had flung ink onto it. Slocum was surprised to see the dark come on so quickly, and with it, a chill that seeped through his skin and into his bones.

"It's just up ahead," Lucy said, as if reading his thoughts.

"I'll have to take your word for it," Slocum said.

"I know. We just barely made it. But we won't have any trouble. I know the way."

She guided her horse off the road and they descended into an even darker place, almost a gully, but it was nestled up close to the mountain on their right. To the left, he could barely discern a wide, yucca-and-pinyon-tree-studded valley. The Joshua trees looked like figures or statues of men.

"We'll have to build a fire right away," Lucy said. "There should be wood there."

She rode on a little farther and then dismounted, tying

her reins to a small tree that he thought might have been an alder. He followed suit, dismounting and finding a place to tie the horses until he could hobble them for the night. He heard a bubbling sound and saw that Lucy had walked a little way ahead and was squatting down.

"This," she said, "is Whiskey Springs."

Slocum walked over and saw where the springs bubbled up out of the rock. As he looked down, Lucy leaned over and lifted a large flat rock. She pulled something out and held it up in the fast-waning light.

"What's that?" he asked.

Lucy laughed. "Take a swig," she said, handing him the object.

Slocum took the bottle, pulled the cork from it and lowered his head to sniff its contents. The pungent aroma of straight whiskey wafted to his nostrils. It smelled good and his mouth watered even as his throat felt suddenly dry.

"Whiskey," he said.

"Go," Lucy said, "take a swallow. That's what it's here for."

Slocum poured some of the whiskey into his mouth, held it there for a moment as he savored its flavor. Then, he swallowed and felt its warmth spread through his belly.

"That's good bourbon," he said. "Did you leave it here?"

"No, but I've got a fresh bottle in my saddlebags that I bought in Victor. May I have a swallow?"

"Oh, I'm sorry. Sure." Slocum handed her the bottle and watched as Lucy took a healthy swig.

"That's why they call this place 'Whiskey Springs,' " she said. "Travelers going up and down the mountain always leave a bottle of whiskey here for the next visitor. In the cold months, many a prospector has welcomed this gift from a stranger."

"It's a good custom," Slocum said and took another swallow after Lucy handed the bottle back to him. With that, he began to strip his two horses of saddles and hobbled them as Lucy gathered firewood. Soon, they had a good, small fire going that helped to ward off the chill flowing down the mountain and into their small canyon.

Lucy laid out their bedrolls and made a pot of coffee, boiled dried beef and vegetables in a small pot. "We'll have to eat out of the same pot," she said. "I didn't bring plates."

"Smells good," Slocum said.

While Lucy cooked, Slocum walked around the spring and along the road. There was concealment where they were. Unless someone knew about the spring, they'd have trouble finding it if they just rode by on the road. The little gully went quite a ways and then rose up to join the flat. Even in the dark, Slocum could see signs that men had used this place quite a bit. He even saw pick marks in the limestone and rock that showed him someone had prospected that particular place.

"Grub's ready," Lucy called, and Slocum's stomach churned with hunger as he retraced his steps back to their camp under the shadow of the bluff.

"Smells good," he repeated as he sat down on a flat rock.

"Pour yourself some coffee, John. Then dig in to this humble stew."

"I could eat the south end of a horse going north," Slocum said.

Lucy laughed.

They ate without hurry, and the coffee was hot and strong as Slocum put away the fare and admired Lucy's beauty in the firelight.

"This was quite a day," Lucy said as she cleaned the pot with sand and some water from the spring.

"It was full enough."

"Now you can tell me about that Williams. Who sent him to kill you?"

"He wasn't sent to kill me, Lucy."

"Well, he was sure trying hard enough."

"Lawton sent him to kill you."

Lucy gasped. "You're not joshing, are you, John?"

"Nope. That's what he told me. I'm just wondering what Lawton has against you."

"Well, he's in with that same bunch."

"Do you think he had a part in killing your father?"

"He could have. He would know who did. Sid has his finger in every pie up in Holcomb Valley. He's as crooked as a snake."

"Well, it doesn't look as if we'll get a warm welcome when we go up there. Maybe you'd better not come with me."

"I'm not afraid of Sid Lawton or anyone else," she said, but Slocum detected a quaver in her voice.

"If your father couldn't stand up against them, what makes you think you can?" Slocum asked.

"Because I've got something that makes them afraid of me."

"Oh? What's that?"

"Evidence. In a safe place."

"Evidence of what?"

"Of other killings. Some of which Sid Lawton was involved in. Murders. And theft of gold mines."

"But not your father's murder?"

Lucy shook her head. "I'm still working on that. But I'll find out the truth. With your help, I hope."

"With no witnesses . . ."

"I think there was a witness to my father's murder. In fact, I'm almost sure of it."

"What makes you say that?" Slocum asked.

"I went over the ground where my father was first attacked. It was on the other side of Belleville. He was dragged clear to the road coming up from the Mojave Desert, where this one goes, to the hanging tree."

"The hanging tree?"

"It's really a double-trunked juniper," she said, "a big tree where several men have been hanged in Holcomb Valley."

"Okay," Slocum said.

"When I went over the ground on the other side of Belleville, I saw fresh tracks behind some bushes and a tree. Someone stood there and watched the whole thing."

"What kind of tracks?"

"They were boot tracks. Small. Either a young boy or a woman witnessed my father being beat up and having a rope put around his neck. I saw that whoever had stood there had run away, back to town, but in a roundabout way."

"Were you able to follow the tracks to see where they went?"

Lucy shook her head. "By the time I followed them to town, they disappeared in a maze of other tracks. Since then I've been looking around, hoping to see some sign of recognition in someone's eyes when they see me."

"And have you?" Slocum asked.

"No, not yet. But I'll find the person who witnessed my father's murder. Then I'll have the evidence I need to bring Chadwick and Lawton, if he's involved, to justice."

"Sounds like a tall order, Lucy."

"Maybe. But I'll never give up."

"It appears that your constable, Lawton, knows that."

"I'm sure he does. But even if he kills me, he can't win."

"Because of that evidence you have squirreled away?"

"Yes. I've told the person who has it hidden for me to bring it out in the open if anything happens to me."

"What if Lawton finds out who's holding that evidence?" Slocum asked.

"I don't even want to think about that, John. It's just too horrible to consider."

"Well, you can bet that Lawton and the others involved in your father's death are prepared to meet any threat to their freedom. They've already proved that they won't hesitate to kill anyone who gets in their way."

Lucy shivered as if a sudden chill had come over her. "That's what scares me," she said.

"I could use another taste of that bourbon," Slocum said as he dug in his pocket for a cheroot.

Lucy passed him the bottle after taking a sip herself. Slocum lit his cheroot in the fire, drawing deeply to bring the smoke into his lungs. He blew it out and took a swallow of the whiskey. Then he leaned back and looked up at the stars. They seemed so close in the clear air of the mountains, and he felt that if he stood on tiptoe, he just might touch one. But that was only an illusion, he knew.

The stars were very far away and were older than anything on earth, he was sure.

"Pretty up there, isn't it?" Lucy asked. "All those stars."

"I never stop wondering about them. How they got there, why they're there."

"To light our way at night, maybe," she said.

"The Indians think the Milky Way is a path to the happy hunting grounds, where they go after they die."

"It's a nice thought," Lucy said. "Anyway, I'm glad we're not down on the desert. I was in dread all day that we'd see a Mojave green."

They let the fire burn low before drinking a last cup of coffee and kissing with whiskey on their breaths.

They made love in their blankets and then slept like people in hibernation, holding on to each other as the coyotes chorused in the hills and the stars winked on and off with a cold, eternal light.

12

Lucy and Slocum awoke to a cold morning. During the night, the fire had died down and both were shivering when they emerged from their bedrolls. Lucy's teeth were chattering until Slocum rekindled the fire and put on a pot of coffee. The sun was not yet over the horizon, but the sky was blue and it promised to be another warm day on the Mojave Desert, and perhaps in the mountains, as well.

"Hungry?" Slocum asked.

"No. I couldn't eat a thing this early."

"Me, neither. As soon as we've had some coffee, let's saddle up."

"Yes," Lucy said. Then, "John, I'm scared."

"Of what?"

"Of going back to Holcomb Valley. Not for myself, but for you."

"Me?"

"Yes. I-I think I'm falling in love with you."

"Hey, whoa, Lucy. Let's not make things any more complicated than they already are."

"I know. It's silly of me, but after last night, and the night before . . ."

Slocum set the coffeepot on a flat rock next to the fire to keep it warm. It had already boiled and the aroma of Arbuckle's finest beans filled the chilly morning air.

"Lucy, look," Slocum said. "In times of danger, people are drawn to each other. It could be a survival trait, but I've seen it before. When there are earthquakes or tornadoes or some kind of natural disaster and a man and a woman wind up together, they often mate and think they're in love. But it's only the situation that caused those feelings."

"Well, I don't think that's it at all. Not with me. You're a very attractive man and I was drawn to you because you're so different from the men I'm used to."

"Different doesn't mean better."

"I know. I can't explain it. But I've gotten sweet on you, John. I can't help it."

"Let's hope it's not a curse," he said and walked over to the horses on the other side of the road to take their hobbles off and put them under saddle.

He grained both horses before he saddled them, and in less than a quarter of an hour, he and Lucy were ready to leave. Before she mounted her horse, she reached into her saddlebag and took out a bottle of whiskey. She placed it under the rock next to the bottle they had drunk from the night before.

"A man could get drunk here real easy," Slocum said.

"I'm sure some have. Shall we go?"

"I'm ready," Slocum said. As they rode away from Whiskey Springs, Slocum looked at the bluff and the gully. There was something peculiar about it, but he couldn't put his finger on it just then. He also looked across the road at the large flat dotted with yucca and a few Joshua trees. There were signs that wagons had run through there and churned up the earth.

"There's been a lot of activity down here," Slocum said to Lucy as they rode past the wide, broad flat. "Any idea why?"

"People come down from Holcomb Valley in the fall to gather pinyon nuts. Like the Serrano Indians once did. Roasted pinyon nuts are very tasty. I'm told the Indians used to grind them into meal, using their *metates*."

"Do they bring wagons down to gather pinyon nuts?"

"I really don't know, John. I suppose if families come down here, they'd ride in wagons."

"Those tracks out there are recent."

"I don't see anything," she said.

"You have to look close, Lucy."

They rode on as the sun rose in the sky and the road got steeper the higher they climbed. They stopped once to heed nature's call, but did not take time to eat.

Finally, the road veered off as they topped the pass and Lucy led the way to the right. Slocum noticed that the road continued on, however. "Where does that lead?" he asked.

"A lake they call Big Bear. The Indians built a dam a long time ago. I think there were once a lot of bears here. I know Holcomb killed a grizzly with his old muzzle-loading rifle. He called it 'Old Smoke.' He discovered gold where he shot the bear."

"And so," Slocum said, "a legend was born."

"Yes, I guess so. We're not far from Holcomb Valley now. In fact, we'll be there in less than an hour."

"I'm looking forward to it," Slocum said dryly.

A while later, Lucy pointed to the twin junipers at the edge of Belleville. There, the road forked again, one leg going left, the other to the right.

"That's the hanging tree," she said. "If you look beyond it, you'll see Octagon House."

Slocum ducked his head to look through the trees. He saw the bare outline of an octagon-shaped building, and as they rode closer he saw carts and wagons, people walking up and down the street. He looked at the hanging tree as they passed it, with its long, twin trunks and green foliage. He could imagine why the double-trunked juniper would be used to hang men. Its position at the very edge of town would serve as a warning that criminals were dealt with harshly in Belleville. But if Lucy was right in her allegations, justice was a sham in Holcomb Valley.

"We can put up at Octagon House," Lucy said. "That's where I've been staying since my father died."

"Is that the only choice?"

"I'm afraid so," she said.

They rode into the small town of Belleville, which, despite its size, seemed to be thriving. Slocum noticed an arrastre near the center of town. A mule was circling it, grinding up rocks hauled in by wagon to extract the gold ore. The machine made a lot of noise, but the townfolk didn't seem to notice. But people did look in their direction as they rode up to the hotel and dismounted. Slocum wrapped the reins of both horses around the hitch rail. He felt the weakness in both legs after riding all morning and he walked a few steps to restore feeling in them.

"They have a boy who will take our horses to the stables and board them," Lucy said, reaching for her bedroll and saddlebags.

Slocum untied the thongs holding his bedroll and shot-gun to his saddle and hefted his saddlebags over his left shoulder. He slid the Winchester from its boot and carried it in his right hand. He and Lucy ascended the steps of the hotel and went inside. She stopped at the desk and Slocum came up behind her and stood there, looking over the lobby and the busy room beyond where people were sitting down to lunch or standing at the long bar.

"You have some messages, Miss Bancroft," the clerk said. He was a thin, short man with balding head. Streamers of hair were stretched across his bare pate and slicked down with wax. He wore a faded string tie and a striped shirt.

"Thanks, Orville," Lucy said. "Mr. John Slocum here would like a room."

"Next to yours?" Orville asked as he handed her a pair of notes he had taken from her box, along with a skeleton key.

"That would be fine," Slocum said just as Lucy opened her mouth to reply.

"Room six," Orville said, handing him a key. "Do you want just one night?"

"It's cheaper by the week or month," Lucy said.

"I'll pay by the night," Slocum said.

"Cash in advance. Be three dollars." Orville reached under the counter and placed the registry book on the counter. "Sign your name here, Mr. Slocum."

Slocum handed Orville three silver dollars and looked at the register. Just above the empty space where he signed his name was a line signed by Alexis Contreras. He didn't see Little Bill's name. He didn't recognize any of the other names.

"Thank you, Mr. Slocum. I'll give you a receipt. Check out time is ten A.M. No loudness after ten P.M.; you're responsible for breakage."

"I'll try and be quiet," Slocum said, taking the key. Orville wrote out a receipt as Lucy stepped aside and read her messages.

"We have horses outside that need boarding," Slocum said.

"I'll have Tim Naylor take them to the stables. You can pay the boarding fee here. It's a dollar a day, includes feed. Currying is six bits extra."

Slocum dug out five more silver dollars, laid them on the counter. "I have two horses and I'll pay Miss Bancroft's fee as well," Slocum said.

Orville made change, but did not give him a receipt.

"I'll put a receipt in your box, Mr. Slocum, after Tim takes care of your horses. He's at lunch now, but it won't be long."

"Fine," Slocum said. "I don't want them to fry out there in the sun under saddle."

"They will be taken care of promptly, Mr. Slocum." Orville turned away from the counter and put the register underneath before walking to the back room.

Slocum and Lucy walked up the stairs together. Slocum could feel Orville's gaze on his back as he ascended the stairs. He turned and saw that Orville was back at the counter, staring up at him. He quickly avoided Slocum's gaze and turned his head in the opposite direction. Lucy was very quiet, which he thought was unusual. She clutched the messages in her hand.

"Bad news?" he asked when they reached the top of the stairway.

"I-I don't know," she said. "Let me show you your room and then take you to mine."

"All right," Slocum said.

Slocum threw his gear just inside the door of the room and walked next door with Lucy. She opened the door. Her room was as spare as his was, except that it looked lived in, but just barely. There was a vase of dying flowers on the chest of drawers, a wardrobe in the corner, a small table and two chairs, a bed. A wash basin and a porcelain pitcher stood on another small table.

"Well, this is my room," she said. "Such as it is."

"Are you hungry?" he asked.

"I am, but I want to freshen up first. Do you want to meet me in the dining room?"

"All right. Give me fifteen minutes."

"Do you want to hear what those messages were about?" she asked.

"If you want to tell me, sure."

"One was not signed. Here, take a look."

Slocum took the scrap of paper Lucy handed him and scanned the hastily scrawled message. It was written in pencil and there was no signature, as Lucy had said. "YOU'LL BE SORRY YOU CAME BACK TO TOWN. GET OUT BEFORE IT'S TOO LATE."

"This looks pretty serious," Slocum said.

"Yes, but maybe not as serious as the other one."

She handed the note to Slocum who read it carefully. His forehead knitted into furrows. The note read: "Lucy, as soon as you get back, meet me after lunch behind the post office. Very important." It was signed "Betsy."

"Betsy's your friend you told me about," Slocum said.

"Yes. She wouldn't send me a note like this unless it was extremely important. John, I'm worried."

"Why?"

"I don't know if I ought to tell you or not."

"Why not?"

"Just because."

"We could play this kid's game all day, Lucy."

"Maybe I'll tell you after I see Betsy."

"Will she be working in the dining room now?"

"Yes, but she won't be able to talk there."

"Fine. When you want to take me into your confidence, Lucy, I'll be more than willing to listen."

"Thanks, John. I'm sorry to be so secretive. But it's necessary right now. One of these days I'll tell you everything. I promise."

"I won't hold my breath," Slocum said.

He heard the door close behind him as he walked to his room. He hadn't locked his door, but he had closed it. He saw now that it was slightly opened.

Slocum drew his Colt and pushed the door open, while standing to one side in case someone inside wanted to take a shot at him. The door creaked as it swung open. He saw no one at first, then stepped inside for a better look.

"I was wondering what happened to you," a voice said.

Slocum whirled and looked in the direction of the voice.

"I hope you're not going to shoot me," the woman said.

"I might. Who in hell are you, and what are you doing in my room?"

Slocum asked the question, but he knew very well who the woman was who stood next to his bed holding a bottle of Kentucky bourbon in her hand.

13

Alexis Contreras smiled and held out the bottle of bourbon.

"I thought you might like a drink after your long ride," she said. "I'm Alexis. And you're the famous John Slocum."

"I'm busy," Slocum said. "And you're trespassing."

"Oh, Mr. Slocum, please. Surely you can grant me a few moments. I have a proposition for you. But first, would you mind closing your door?"

Slocum looked at the woman he had seen only from a distance the day before, riding with Little Bill hell-bent-for-leather. He was not prepared for her now. Her beauty was startling. She had finely chiseled cheekbones, a patrician nose, long blond hair that caressed her shoulders like a shawl of the finest silk, bright green eyes and lips that seemed to promise much more than they would ever say out loud.

Slocum closed the door and holstered his pistol. "I don't have much time," he said. "So make it short."

"Don't you want to have a drink with me?"

Slocum licked his dry lips as Alexis walked across the room to the table. She set the bottle down and took a couple of glasses from the top of the bureau that were on a tray with the water pitcher and bowl.

"I suppose I have time for a taste," he said.

"Straight, or do you want water with it?" Alexis opened the bottle, pulling the cork with her teeth. She set the cork down and lifted the bottle to pour. "It's Old Taylor," she said.

"Straight is fine."

"Come on over and sit down, Mr. Slocum. I won't bite you."

"Oh, I think you would bite me," he said.

"Well, not before we get to know each other."

Slocum pulled out a chair and sat down on the opposite side of the table where he could watch her. She poured the two glasses half full of bourbon and slid one across to him. She put one foot up on the chair and leaned over toward him. She wore a dress that hiked up her leg and revealed part of her inner thigh.

"Here's to a beneficial partnership," she said, offering her glass in a toast.

"Partnership? Aren't you jumping to a great big conclusion?"

"Oh, I don't know. Wait'll you hear what I have to say."

"Maybe you should propose that toast after I hear what you have to say."

"Well, then, let's toast to the beginning of a beautiful friendship."

Slocum picked up his glass and clunked it against hers.

She smiled and something inside him melted. Then she drained her glass without batting an eye or shedding a tear. Slocum drank one swallow and felt the whiskey burn all the way down to his toes.

"Friendship is a funny thing," he said. "You can't buy it and you can't sell it. But it's worth a hell of a lot."

"I agree," she said, and sat down in the chair. "And I don't take friendship lightly."

"What is this proposition you mentioned?" he asked.

"I have a job offer for you, Mr. Slocum. You'll go to work for Mr. Chadwick. In addition, you'll be paid in full for your mules."

"Then you admit that Chadwick stole my mules," Slocum said.

"Let's say that Luke Chadwick knows your mules were stolen from you and is willing to pay for them as an inducement for you to work for him."

"What kind of work would that be?"

"I'm sure Mr. Chadwick will tell you. If you're interested, I'll arrange for you two to meet."

"When?"

"This afternoon, if you wish."

"I'd be very interested in meeting with Luke Chadwick."

"Then you will take the job?"

"I'll talk to him, and make my decision then. Fair enough?"

"I suppose so," Alexis said.

Slocum pushed his glass away and started to get up from the table. Alexis, pouting, got up, too. "What are you going to do?" she asked.

"I'm going to lunch," he said. "And you're going to see Chadwick and give him my answer."

"But must you leave so soon, Mr. Slocum?"

"Yes. I promised."

"You know," she said, moving around the table toward him, "you're a very attractive man, Mr. Slocum."

Slocum said nothing.

Alexis moved close to him and put her arms over his shoulders. She was tall enough so that she didn't have to stand on tiptoe. "Very attractive," she purred, as she pooched out her lips invitingly.

Slocum turned his head away from her in rejection of her advances, but this seemed to infuriate Alexis. She ringed her arms around Slocum's neck and drew his lips down to hers. She kissed him with a passion that stirred the dead coals of desire deep inside him. She pried apart his teeth with her tongue and he felt it slither inside his mouth like some warm-blooded creature.

He felt his resolve melt like butter in the intense heat of her kiss. She reached down with one hand and grabbed his cock and balls and kneaded them like dough. Her fingers felt like soft lightning bolts shooting electricity into him. He became aroused instantly, his cock swelling with engorged blood, stiffening in her hands until it was rock hard, rigid as an iron pole.

"You have time," she whispered when she broke the kiss. "We both have time. I want you now, John Slocum, and from what I feel down there, you want me, too."

Slocum opened his mouth to protest, but Alexis planted her lips on his once again and worked magic with her tongue inside his mouth. He grabbed her then and drew her against him until she released her hold on his balls and shoved her cunt up against his hard cock. He could almost feel it beneath the cloth of her dress and the fabric of his trousers.

"Take me," she whispered. "Take me now."

Alexis began to unbutton her blouse. Slocum took off his frock coat and unbuckled his gun belt. He sat on a chair and took off his boots and was shedding shirt and trousers when Alexis peeled her panties off and stood before him nude. He swallowed and went to her, lifting her from the floor and carrying her to the bed. He laid her down and slid next to her. She grabbed him with both arms and began kissing his face, neck and ears.

"You won't be sorry," she husked in his ear as he plied her cunt with the middle finger of his left hand. He felt her warm juices flow over his finger and he pressed hard against her cunt as she began to thrust her hips upward and back down, undulating with the movement of his finger.

"That feels so good," she said and grabbed his cock and pulled on it, squeezing it until he could feel the blood pounding in his temples.

"Hurry, hurry," she said, and Slocum removed his finger and climbed atop her. Her hair flowed like a blond fan over the covered pillow as he lowered himself to her. She put the head of his cock at the portals of her cunt and thrust her hips upward. He slid his cock inside her and swathed it in the wet warmth of her steaming cunt.

He slid his prick in and out of her as she writhed and bucked beneath him, her eyes glazed with passion. He could smell the musk of her that mixed with the faint perfume she wore. She was a woman who wanted to be ridden hard and Slocum drove into her with all the lust she stirred up in him.

"Good, good," she moaned. "I like it like that. Hard and fast."

Slocum said nothing, but gripped her hips in his hands and took her under his control. He plumbed her depths with his prick and the bed rocked and creaked as the slats groaned under their weight and movement.

"Yes, yes," Alexis breathed, and he felt her buck with multiple climaxes as if a bomb had burst inside her. Still, Slocum held back, willing himself to outlast her.

"You're quite a man," Alexis said. "Any other would have come in the first ten seconds."

"You talk too much," he said and kissed her on the lips, just to taste that tongue of hers again.

Alexis went into convulsive spasms as she climaxed again and again. She seemed in the grip of madness as her eyes rolled back in their sockets.

"Now, now," she screamed, "let me have it all."

Slocum thought the bed would break as he pounded into her, and even with his hands on her hips, he could not keep her from trying to consume him. He raced with her to the top of her next climax, and, in a sudden burst of seed, exploded his balls and poured inside her like a volcano erupting.

It was then that Alexis experienced her strongest orgasm, screaming with delight and shuddering all over as if she had been electrified. Her spasms lasted for several moments as Slocum, panting, fought for oxygen and some regularity in his breathing.

"Oh," Alexis sighed. "That was most wonderful. Thank you, Mr. Slocum, thank you, thank you."

"You might as well call me John," he said, as he slid from her sweat-soaked body and lay on his back.

At that moment the door opened and he realized he had forgotten to lock it.

Lucy stepped into the room and gasped in startled amazement. Slocum blinked, caught by surprise.

"John," Lucy gasped. "How could you?"

Alexis arose and looked at Lucy, a wry smile on her lips.

"Well," Alexis said, "if it isn't Miss Bancroft. Care to join us, honey?"

"Oh, you, you . . ." Lucy exclaimed and turned around, slamming the door behind her.

"She seemed a little peeved," Alexis said.

"Well, you know women," Slocum said.

"Not as well as you do, I suspect. So, you've been sparking that little tart, have you?"

"I don't think we need to talk about Lucy Bancroft," Slocum said.

"No, we don't. I'll meet you at the hotel this afternoon, around three o'clock, and take you out to meet Mr. Chadwick."

Slocum said nothing. He watched as Alexis arose from the bed and put her clothes back on. She patted her hair and walked out of the room, closing the door behind her.

Slocum lay there for several moments. The room was so empty, he wondered if he had imagined everything that had happened. But no, he could still smell the faint perfume and the musk and the coverlet on the bed looked as if it had been hit by a cyclone.

It was too bad, he thought, that Lucy had to walk in when she did. But it couldn't be helped. She didn't own him, but he was sure she was upset by what she had seen.

Slocum dressed slowly, trying to think of some comforting words to say to Lucy when he saw her. He supposed she was in the dining room, fuming, mad as hell, but waiting for him to join her.

Slocum walked down the stairs and entered the dining room. He looked all around, but there was no sign of Lucy. Nor did he see any face he knew. He sat down at a table and ordered from the bill of fare.

He was just finishing up his lunch when the hotel clerk entered the dining room. Slocum watched as the man made his way to his table.

"You looking for me?" Slocum asked.

"I have a message for you, Mr. Slocum."

"What is it?"

"Miss Bancroft sent the stable boy up to ask if you would meet her there. Right away."

"If you'll direct me to the stables, I'll do that," Slocum said.

He paid his bill and walked out onto the street. The stables were on the other side of the small town, less than three blocks away.

He wondered why Lucy had sent for him, and what she was doing at the stables. He also wondered what had happened that made her skip lunch.

People looked at Slocum as he walked down the main street, following the clerk's directions. There wasn't much to the town, a land office, a small hardware store, a mercantile and a feed store. He could hear the arrastre grinding and by the time he reached the end of the street, he saw people running towards the stables.

Slocum started running, too.

14

Slocum arrived at the stables to find a small crowd gathering out in front of the large barn. People were talking in low tones and he couldn't hear what they were saying.

"What happened?" Slocum asked a bonneted woman at the edge of the crowd.

"I think someone's been killed," she said.

"Man or woman?"

"A woman, I think."

Slocum's heart sank as he thought of Lucy. There was a price on her head, he knew.

He made his way through the crowd, shoving people aside, until he saw what they were all gawking at.

There, on the ground, lay a young woman, her blouse covered with blood, her face turned away from him so that he could not see if she were dead or alive.

Bending over her, and weeping, was another woman, one he recognized. It was Lucy, and she was sobbing so much that her shoulders shook.

Slocum walked up to Lucy and put a hand on her shoulder. She looked up at him, tears streaming down her face.

"Oh, John, look what they've done," Lucy said, her voice quavering with emotion.

"Is that your friend? Betsy?" Slocum asked.

Lucy shook her head. "No, it-it's not Betsy, but . . ."

She stopped talking and looked at the man who had stepped up to stand beside Slocum. Slocum turned his head to see who had startled her.

The man was tall and angular, with deep-sunk pale-gray eyes that seemed to flicker with shadows. He wore a dark-blue shirt that sported a badge over the left pocket. His clothing was neatly pressed. He had a thick, brushy moustache, flecked with gray, like his long, straight hair, that curved down his chin on both sides in the shape of a horseshoe. He had high, sharp cheekbones and a thin slit of a mouth. He was nearly as tall as Slocum, and wore a Smith & Wesson .38 holstered on his wide belt. His shiny black boots were covered with a thin patina of dust.

"What happened here?" the man said. Then he looked at Lucy. "Did you kill this woman?"

"I—no, I-I found her like this," Lucy said.

The man turned to Slocum.

"How about you, mister? Do you know who murdered this girl?"

"I have no idea," Slocum said. "I just came here myself."

The man turned around and spoke to the crowd. "Unless you have business here, or know who did this, clear out. Now."

He spoke softly, but his voice carried and it was laden with authority. The crowd began to disperse. Then the tall man turned back to Slocum.

"I don't know your face," he said. "I'm Sid Lawton, constable of Holcomb Valley."

"John Slocum. I just rode in this morning."

"Well, Mr. Slocum, maybe you'd better explain why you're here and your connection with the slain woman."

"Sid," Lucy said, getting to her feet, "I asked Mr. Slocum to meet me here." She wiped away her tears.

"Miss Bancroft, it looks to me like you're in a lot of trouble. And Slocum, you are, too, unless you can explain any of this."

"I can explain," Lucy said quickly. "I went to meet my friend Betsy at the post office. She wasn't there, but someone said they had seen her heading toward the stables. I walked over here, heard a scream from inside and saw Constance come staggering out. She collapsed a few minutes ago and by the time I got to her she was dead."

"Did she say anything before she died?" Lawton asked.

Lucy shook her head. Too quickly, Slocum thought.

"This is Constance Waller?" Lawton asked. "The girl who works at the mercantile?"

"Yes, she and Betsy were, are, friends of mine," Lucy said.

Lawton squatted and examined the dead woman. She appeared to be about twenty-two years old, with sandy hair and what had been a pretty face. She had a hole in her chest that appeared to be from a knife wound. Lawton turned her over and Slocum saw at least two more stab wounds in her back. One appeared to be deep, while the other was more of a slash and didn't appear to have been the cause of death.

Lawton stood up and looked Slocum up and down.

"I've got a report in my office on you, Slocum," the

constable said. "I think you're the man who murdered my nephew and my cousin in Victor a couple of days ago."

"The report is wrong," Slocum said.

"I can arrest you, however. What do you think of that?"

"Not much," Slocum said. "Your nephew tried to kill me. I acted in self-defense. Miss Bancroft here was a witness."

"Is that true, Miss Bancroft?" Lawton asked.

"Yes, it is. Harry and Ralph tried to kill Mr. Slocum, and me, too. Mr. Slocum shot both men while defending me and himself."

"Still, it's a very serious charge. I could hold you both in jail until it's all sorted out."

"Lawton," Slocum said, "I came here because two men, named Beddoes and Deakins, stole twenty of my mules and drove them here. They killed my partner. If you're going to arrest anyone, I suggest you start with those two. Unless they have a bill of sale for those twenty mules, they're guilty of theft, and there are people in Victor who can testify that they murdered my friend, Tad Foster, in cold blood."

Lawton looked at Slocum with those pale dead eyes and said nothing for several moments.

"What he's telling you is all true," Lucy said. "I watched his friend die from shotgun wounds."

"And what is your testimony worth, Miss Bancroft? You've been nothing but trouble since your father died in that accident."

Lucy bit her lip to keep from saying something she might regret later on. Instead, she just glared at Lawton, her lips quivering in rage.

"If you don't have solid evidence against me or Miss

Bancroft, I don't think you have grounds to arrest either of us," Slocum said.

"Maybe not. But I'll give you fair warning, Slocum. If you leave town before I've finished my investigation, I'll track you down and we'll see if you might decorate our hanging tree here in Holcomb Valley."

"Is that a threat?" Slocum asked.

"Mind your p's and q's, Slocum. It's a warning from a duly elected officer of the peace."

"I'll take it as a threat," Slocum said.

Lawton's eyes narrowed, but he said nothing just then. Slocum sensed a dangerous man facing him, one who would not back down in a fight. He also suspected that Sid Lawton was much more than a peace officer. He appeared to be a man who thought of himself as judge, jury and executioner.

"Sid, will you please see that someone takes care of Constance? I don't want her to lie out here for everybody to stare at."

"I'll do my duty," Lawton said curtly. "Don't you go nowhere, neither, ma'am. I think I'll have some questions for you when I find out all the facts about my nephew's and my cousin's deaths."

"I'm not going anywhere," Lucy said, almost defiantly, as she sidled next to Slocum. "But I've been telling you the truth."

"We'll see," Lawton said and turned his back on the two. "Someone bring me a sheet or a blanket," he yelled to the few onlookers who had remained some distance away.

Lucy grabbed Slocum's arm at the elbow and pulled

him away from Lawton. "Let's get out of here," she said. "There's something I've got to tell you."

They walked back to the main street in Belleville and before they reached the hotel, Lucy pulled him between two buildings where they could not be easily seen from the street.

"If you're going to jump on me about that woman . . ." Slocum started to say.

"No, that's the least of my worries right now, John. I've got to tell you what happened and why I'm worried."

"All right," he said.

"I was going to have lunch at the hotel. I looked for Betsy, but she wasn't there. Then, Constance, Constance Waller, she came up and told me that Betsy wouldn't be behind the post office, but wanted me to meet her at the stables."

"Why?" Slocum asked.

"Constance said Betsy was going to leave town and had something important to tell me."

"So, you went with Constance to the stables?"

"Yes. But, before we got there, Constance saw someone at the stables who scared her. She started running and before I could get my wits about me, she went inside. By the time I got there, she was badly hurt."

"Did you see who stabbed her?"

"No, but it was someone Constance knew. She said, before she ran off, 'That's the man Betsy is scared of.' "

"Anything else?"

"Yes, as she ran away, she said, 'My God, maybe he's killed her.' "

Slocum frowned. He watched people pass by on the street but none looked in their direction. Somewhere, he heard a dog bark, followed by a woman's voice yelling for the dog to be quiet.

"Did she die before she could say anything to you?" Slocum asked.

"She could barely talk, but she said three words. And then she died."

"What did she say?"

"She said, 'Betsy.' Then, she barely managed to say 'Pygmy Cabin.' "

"Pygmy cabin? Do you know what that means?" Slocum asked.

"I-I think so," Lucy said. "A long time ago one of the early prospectors must have had to put up shelter real quick. Off in the woods, there's a small cabin made of logs. It's just high enough off the ground to crawl into. You can't stand up in it and it has no doors or windows. I've seen it, and the folks around here got to calling it Pygmy Cabin."

"Why would your friend Betsy go there?"

"I have no idea," Lucy said. "But I'm going to saddle up my horse and ride out there after dark."

"Maybe I'll go with you," Slocum said. "I've got something to do this afternoon. Wait for me at the hotel."

"What have you got to do?" Lucy asked.

"I don't think I should tell you."

"Why? Does it have something to do with Alexis?"

Slocum said nothing.

"It does, doesn't it?" Lucy said.

"Let's just say I'm going to meet Luke Chadwick this afternoon. Maybe I can get a line on what happened to your father."

"Is this about your mules?"

"Yes, it is."

"I'll bet Alexis has something to do with it," Lucy said.

"Just wait for me. And stay out of trouble this afternoon."

"Aren't you going back to the hotel?"

"Yes, later. There's something I have to do first."

"And you're not going to tell me what that is, are you?"

"No, Lucy. The less you know about what I do from now on, the better off you'll be."

"I see. So, I'm not the only one guilty of keeping secrets, am I?"

"I guess not. Sometimes secrets are necessary."

Lucy pouted for a moment, then summoned some inner resolve. She raised her head and held it high.

"I'll see you tonight, then," she said.

"Yes. I promise."

Slocum watched Lucy walk out onto the street. Then he went the other way and came out on the street behind the main one. Like the others, most of the buildings were hewn out of logs and well chinked with mud. Log cabins were strewn all around the meadow that was called Belleville. It looked, he thought, like a temporary town. A town that, one day soon, would end up empty, a ghost town, like so many he had seen in the West.

People came westward to find their dreams and sometimes they stopped in a place that was no good. There, they lost all their money and possessions and either were killed or died, or moved away.

Slocum felt that Belleville was that kind of town, one built on greed, and so isolated from the rest of civilization, it was doomed and would die one day and become nothing but a ghost town, full of whispers and secrets no one would ever know.

15

Slocum walked a roundabout way back to the far side of the stables. He wanted to see if he was being followed, and he wanted to watch what was happening with the dead girl without being seen. It took him the better part of a half an hour to reach his goal.

But he knew that no one had followed him, and by the time he got to the rear of the stables, they had removed the body of Constance and the gawkers had all gone. Still, he waited, standing in a small thicket of young pines and junipers, watching the barn from a vantage point that afforded him a view of the stables both in front and in back.

He did not have to wait long. A young man soon appeared, emerging through the back doors of the stables, carrying a wooden bucket. He dipped the bucket into a wooden tank that was stream-fed, filled it, then went back into the stables.

But, while the young man was filling the bucket, he had looked all around as if checking to see if anyone was looking. Slocum had not moved, and he stood in deep shadow, his black frock coat just a darker shade amid the trees.

Slocum leaned against a sturdy pine for support as he continued to stand stock-still, waiting.

A few moments later, a man rode out of the stables, again from the rear, and he kept a straight course that concealed him from the town of Belleville. The man's shirt, a light blue cloth, appeared to be splotched with blood. He rode slowly, but deliberately, until he disappeared in the pines.

Slocum waited there another fifteen minutes before he left his place of concealment and walked to the stables. He heard noises from inside, a shuffling, a clattering and a swishing.

When he entered the stables, the boy was tossing hay into a feed bin. The boy jumped a foot when he saw Slocum.

"You got a name?" Slocum asked.

"Yeah. It's, I mean, I'm Rodney Cole."

The boy was still wet behind the ears, a towheaded youth of about eighteen or nineteen, with jug ears that stuck out like handles, peach fuzz on his chin, wildly darting brown eyes, thin as a rail. He was also very nervous.

"That's my horse you're throwing hay to," Slocum said.

"Yes, sir, it, he just come in today. Mighty nice horse, too. Ain't never seen one like him."

"I want to know what Little Bill was doing here."

"Little Bill?"

"Yeah, you know who I mean. He just rode out of here on a black Arabian with a white blaze and a shaved topknot."

"Oh, that feller. Yeah, he rented that horse from me. It belongs to Miss Alexis."

"Do you know what Little Bill was doing here?" Slocum asked.

"No, sir, he was here when I come back from lunch. They was a gal killed right out front and I didn't get to see none of it."

"Did you know the girl?"

"I seen her a time or two. I didn't know her."

"So you weren't here when she was stabbed to death?"

"No, sir. I don't know nothin' about it."

"Do you know where Little Bill was going?"

"I reckon he was goin' back over to Union Flat. That's where the bunch is holed up."

"The bunch?" Slocum asked.

"Well, I camp over there myself, and there's a bunch what has diggins there, Beddoes and Deakins and some others who come into town ever so often and raise hell."

"But Little Bill asked you to look out back for him, didn't he?"

Cole blinked and swallowed. "He asked me to see if there was anybody out back. Said he didn't want to run into nobody when he left."

"Didn't you think that was odd?" Slocum asked.

"Yessir, I did, but he give me two dollars just to walk out back and fill me a bucket with water."

"Saddle up that Palouse, Rodney, and I'll give you two dollars to keep your mouth shut about me being here."

"Why, shore, mister. Easiest money I ever made."

Ten minutes later, Slocum was following Little Bill's track as it arrowed through to the pines, then angled off into small mounds that bordered the town of Belleville, little hillocks that blended into the steeper hills.

Slocum followed the tracks where they cut through the hillocks and emerged on a higher plateau. He could catch glimpses of Belleville as he followed Little Bill's path. It gave him a clearer picture of the town and its scattered log cabins. It looked, he thought, more like a frontier settlement than an organized town site. The roads were just wide paths, rutted over the years. Belleville looked as if it had just been slapped together after Bill Holcomb made his strike, the town populated by people with picks and pans and sluice boxes who endured the hardships of the mountains hoping to strike it rich.

The tracks led to a road through the woods, a winding road through jumbles of rocks and outcroppings. Finally, Slocum heard voices ahead. He stopped and dismounted, tied the Palouse to a sturdy juniper branch and walked toward the sound of men talking. He used the rocks and trees for cover and sought higher ground. He stepped carefully so that he would not make noise.

Through the trees, he saw what appeared to be a camp, with some structures and canvas tents. He circled so that he came to a place in the rocks that overlooked the site where the men were gathered.

He crawled to a spot among the rocks where he could look down on the camp and not be seen. He peered down through the piled up rocks and saw a small log house, some hitch rails, sluice boxes, pans, picks, axes and five men squatted around a smoldering fire talking among themselves.

He recognized Little Bill right away. He had removed his shirt and was dipping it into a cast-iron pot on the fire that was full of boiling water. He glanced at the other men.

Beddoes was sitting on a stump, smoking a cigarette. Deakins was there, too, sitting on the ground, his back against a pine tree. There was no sign of the mules, but there were three small but sturdy wagons lined up some distance away from the camp.

Slocum could not hear what the men were saying. There was another man there he did not know, but the fifth man, who stood in their midst, was none other than Sid Lawton, who was speaking in low tones to Little Bill.

Slocum's stomach knotted when he saw Deakins and Beddoes. The anger rose up in him like a clenched fist and it was all he could do not to draw his pistol and call the two out.

But Slocum knew he was badly outnumbered and would stand little chance against five armed men. He knew where their camp was, though, and vowed to return at a later time to confront those two. Seeing Lawton there, he was sure there would be no justice dealt to Little Bill. Slocum was convinced that he was the man who had killed Constance and there was no question that Lawton knew all about that murder.

Slocum started to crawl backward when he felt something hard strike him in the back, near his lowest ribs.

"You just hold it right there, mister," a voice said and Slocum's blood froze.

He felt a hand snake his pistol from its holster and he stiffened, his mind racing. He was sure now that what he had felt was a gun barrel sticking him in the back.

"You're on my claim, mister, and if you make one quick move, you're a dead man."

Then Slocum heard the click of a lock as the man speaking to him cocked his rifle. The harsh metallic sound sent a shiver up Slocum's spine and he wondered if this was his time to die.

16

Slocum thought of his belly gun and wondered if he could reach it before the man behind him squeezed the trigger of his rifle. He waited for his chance, wondering how he had been so careless as to let someone get the drop on him.

"Just turn around real slow, mister, so I can get a look at you."

Slocum turned over and saw the man with the rifle. He did not recognize him. The man appeared to be in his forties, with a full beard, thick moustache. He wore a battered felt hat that was stained with various substances. He held a rifle aimed straight at Slocum's belly. He had the Colt stuck in behind his belt.

"You got yourself a belly gun, I see. Fork it over. Real easy now."

"Look, if I'm on your claim, I didn't know it," Slocum said. "I'd like to correct that by leaving right now."

"Fork over that belly gun, butt first, son."

Slocum reached down, his hand moving very slowly,

131

and pulled the pistol out of his waistband. He handed it to the man, who snickered and stuck the pistol in his pocket.

"Now, ease on back down and stand up. We'll go somewheres where we can talk and you can tell me what you're doing sneaking around up here on my claim."

Slocum scooted down the slope of the hillock and stood up. The man motioned with his rifle in the direction he wanted Slocum to walk. Slocum kept walking and realized they were headed to the place where he had tied the Palouse.

"That's far enough. Them jaspers back there can't hear us now."

Slocum turned around and looked at the man with the rifle. His clothing was filthy, embedded with dirt, as were his hands.

"I seen you ride up and sneak over behind them rocks to spy on Beddoes and them. What for?"

"Beddoes and Deakins killed a friend of mine, in Victor," Slocum said. "And I was tracking Little Bill. I think Little Bill murdered a girl in town this morning."

"What's your name, stranger?" the miner asked.

"Slocum. John Slocum."

"Was you the sharpshooter who rode with Quantrill?"

"Maybe. Why do you ask?"

" 'Cause I was sent to Quantrill, too, same as you. Don't you recognize me, John?"

"Not right off."

"Why, I'm Sam Coberly. 'Course I was just a kid, then, same as you, a mite thinner. But now I got me three growed sons and it's the onliest way I was able to hold on to my claim here in Holcomb."

"Sammy? Sammy Coberly?"

"The very same. I remember when General Lee made you a courier to General Sterling Price after General Grant whupped ass at Vicksburg."

"Yeah," Slocum said, "and Price promoted me to captain and sent me off to fight with Quantrill."

"Same as me. Lordamighty, what in hell are you doin' way out here?"

"I was delivering some mules to a man in Victor and I got jumped by Beddoes and Deakins down there."

"Ha, that sounds like 'em. Scoundrels, ever' one of 'em. Me, I come back here after the war and it was like burnin' out a nest of rats in the storm cellar. Squatters ever'where and gold fever like crazy. I had to fight for my claim and I'm still fightin' for it. Which was why I come up on you like I did, John. I thought you was just another rascal comin' to beat me out of my claim."

"No. I'm just here to get my money and see that those two men I mentioned are brought to justice. They killed my partner on this trip, a boy, really, who never hurt a fly."

"Until a few minutes ago, Cap'n John, I truly thought you was dead."

"A lot of people thought that," Slocum said.

"I mean when we raided Lawrence, you went down; took a bullet in your innards. We all thought you was dead."

"I was lucky," Slocum said, thinking back to that time when he had lain near death after the raid on Lawrence. It wasn't until the spring of 1866, after the Civil War had ended, that Slocum had recovered enough to travel.

"Here, John, take your guns back," Coberly said, handing the weapons to Slocum.

"Thanks. You got the drop on me, for sure, Sam."

"Did you go back home after that?"

"I went back to Calhoun County, Georgia," Slocum said. "But there was no home there anymore. Not my home, anyway."

"They call this Union Flat," Coberly said, "because this part of the country hated the South and Southerners, and I had to keep fightin' long after my old Sharp's rifle wore out."

"I know what you mean, Sam."

"Well, looky, let's get your horse and I'll take you to my digs and we can catch up on old times."

"I haven't got much time," Slocum said.

"At least meet my three sons. They're good boys and might be able to help you."

"I'd be pleased to meet them," Slocum said. "So long as I get back to Octagon House by three this afternoon."

"Oh, you got plenty of time," Coberly said as Slocum untied the Palouse.

The two men walked on dried brown pine needles down a gradual slope and up another, following a thin ridgeline that dipped into a small meadow. Beyond, Slocum saw a cabin in the pines and heard sounds of hammering in the distance. There was a steep hill behind the cabin that rose up above the pines and was covered with a jumble of rocks.

"That's my place," Coberly said, "and behind it my mine. Me and my boys are hard-rock miners. We dug deep into that hill back there where I've found many a promising vein."

"So, you're making a living," Slocum said.

"At sixteen dollars the ounce, we do right well, but it's hard work. Harder'n sluicin' or pannin'."

"What do you know about Sid Lawton?" Slocum asked, as they approached the cabin.

"As crooked as they come. He runs Belleville, and he's run off a lot of good folk. I don't have no truck with him or his kind."

"I gather you've had men try and jump your claim."

"Yep. That's why you don't see much of us in Belleville. We do our business down the hill in San Bernardino or over in Victor and we do it seldom as we can."

"How do you keep your earnings here a secret?" Slocum asked as he wrapped his reins around a hitching post near the cabin.

"Even that secret's a secret, John. We don't talk much, me and my boys, and we don't show our money to nobody."

"That's wise," Slocum said.

One of the boys emerged from behind the cabin. He was shirtless and brawny, carrying a Sharp's carbine.

"Did you get him, Pa?" the boy asked.

"Jesse, this is an old friend from the war. You come on and shake hands with John Slocum."

Jesse grinned and stuck out a hand as he came up to his father and Slocum.

"*The* John Slocum? Pa has told us many a tale about you and him ridin' with Quantrill."

"That's something I'd like to forget," Slocum said.

"Mighty pleased to meet you," Jesse said.

"Come on, John, and I'll show you the mine. We call

it The Golden Lady. She's been mighty good to us, hasn't she, Jesse?"

"I reckon," Jesse said, before waving good-bye and taking a different path.

"He's on lookout way up yonder in them rocks," Sam explained. "He's the one what spotted you ridin' in here."

"I was tracking Little Bill," Slocum said.

"He's another no-account, like them others."

The mine entrance was concealed by a thick stand of pines, and Slocum saw that Coberly had taken great pains to spread out the tailings so that a casual observer would not be able to tell, at a glance, how much rock and dirt had been taken out of the mine.

Slocum could hear the echoes of hammers ringing on stone. As they stood at the entrance, Coberly gave two loud whistles that sounded like the call of a valley quail. In fact, the call was startling. He had heard quail calling from their perches on the yucca on the drive out to Victor.

The hammers stopped, and soon two stalwart young men appeared at the entrance. Both carried rifles and packed pistols on their belts.

"John, these are my other two sons, Brad and Steve. Boys, shake hands with John Slocum."

The two boys grinned and stepped forward. Both had strong, firm grips as they each shook Slocum's hand. They had long hair like their other brother, wide shoulders, and bulging muscles from their hard work in the mine.

"We've heard a lot about you, Mr. Slocum," Steve said. "Pleased to meet you."

"Likewise," Brad said, his grin as wide as a plate.

"Okay, boys, you can rest for a minute, then get back to work."

"I've got to relieve Jesse pretty quick," Brad said. "He's had enough sun for today."

Sam laughed and slapped Brad on the shoulder. It was plain to Slocum that this was a very close family. He envied them, the brothers especially. His own brother, Robert, had died too young, in the war.

"Well, you know what to do," Sam said. "John here's got to go somewheres, but I'll bet we see him again real soon."

Sam walked Slocum around the hump in the land and told him about the mine. "I have three entrances here," he explained. "Inside, it's like a honeycomb. I have shafts bleeding off one another. As we follow a vein, we make another shaft."

"I didn't see any shoring in your mine," Slocum said.

"No need for none," Sam said. "It's solid rock underneath that hump of mountain. We make the shaft just big enough for one man to pass through at a time, or all of us single file."

"I don't think I could work underground," Slocum said.

Sam laughed. "That's what separates the hard-rock miner from the panners and sluicers. You got to be a mole to work in all that dark."

"I didn't see any lamps," Slocum said.

"Oh, we got lamps, but we know this mine so well, we only use them when we need to, and there's plenty of ventilation with those three shafts."

"And you're following veins all the time?"

Sam showed Slocum another entrance and then they retraced their steps. "I heard tell that when this old earth was formed, it was all fire and brimstone and a great mass of gold was like water, flowing down underneath all the earth and rock and cooling in some spots, turning hard and staying put. Here in Holcomb Valley, they say that underneath is a whole lake of gold. They say that every vein could lead to the Mother Lode."

"It sounds fantastic," Slocum said.

"Well, I believe it. I follow those veins, hoping I'll strike the Mother Lode and be the richest man in the world."

Slocum laughed.

"I hope you do," he said.

Suddenly, they both heard a muffled explosion that shook the ground beneath their feet.

"What was that?" Slocum asked.

"Damned Luke Chadwick. He's been blasting deep underground most ever' danged day. Maybe he's trying to find that lake of gold."

"You know Chadwick?"

"That whole bunch down there works for Luke. He's a thief and a scoundrel."

"Maybe a murderer?"

"That would explain a lot of what's happened up here."

"He's the man I'm going to meet this afternoon."

Sam said nothing, but Slocum could see he was chewing on the information.

They reached the cabin and Sam stuck out his hand. "You'd best be on your way back to Belleville, John," he said. "But you come back. And if you ever need our help, just give me a holler."

"I'll do that, Sam," Slocum said. "And thanks. It's good to run into an old friend way out here."

"You mind your back, now. Hear? 'Specially around Luke Chadwick."

"I will," Slocum said as he climbed onto the Palouse. He waved good-bye and turned his horse back in the direction from where he had come. He followed the same track so he would remember it when it came time to return.

He had a hunch that it would not be long before he would be back. For now, he knew where the enemy was holed up. Right there on Union Flat.

17

Alexis was waiting outside Octagon House when Slocum walked back from the stables. She sat in a small buggy pulled by a roan gelding.

"I was wondering where you were," she said.

"Oh, just walking around," he said.

"Climb in. We don't have far to go. Luke's expecting you."

Slocum climbed into the buggy. Alexis cracked the whip and the roan stepped out. She took the road past the hanging tree at the edge of Belleville, then turned off on a fork that took them through a thick forest of pines.

Slocum noticed that the road winding through the pines was heading in the general direction of Union Flat to the west, but was wending on a northerly course. He was a man who kept his bearings—an old habit of his.

"Luke doesn't live far from town," Alexis said. "This is actually a small valley."

Slocum nodded, but said nothing. He was keeping track

of where they were going in case he needed to come back this way on his own.

The pines began to thin out, and there were large piles and outcroppings of boulders on either side of the road. Soon they entered a clearing, and on the other side, Slocum saw a small cabin nestled in a grove of pines. A man stood outside, as if expecting them.

"There's Luke now," Alexis said, waving. Luke Chadwick did not wave back. He was drawing on a cigarette, which he finished and threw to the ground. He put a boot heel to it and snuffed it out in the dirt.

"Hello, Luke," Alexis said as she pulled on the reins to bring the buggy to a path parallel to the cabin. "This is John Slocum."

"Light down," Chadwick said. He had a deep, gravelly voice that emanated from a wide chest. He stood about five feet nine in his boots, was clean shaven, with dark hair that was cropped short. He wore black trousers that were well cut, and a white shirt that seemed incongruous in such an isolated, woodsy place. He also wore a fancy gun belt studded with silver ornaments. The pistol jutting from the holster was a Colt .44 with a pearl handle. Slocum took him for a dandy, fond of good clothing, but he sensed a hardness in the man that belied his fancy dress.

"Slocum, I'm Luke Chadwick, and I'm glad you came out."

"I'll listen to your offer, Chadwick."

"I hope you'll take me up on it. Come on inside."

Alexis and Slocum followed Chadwick inside the cabin. It was sparsely furnished, with a large, wide bed, a heavy table made out of cedar, matching chairs. There was a bar and small kitchen. Everything in it was neat.

There was a mounted grizzly head on one wall, a deer head on another.

"You two take a seat," Chadwick said. "Whiskey, Slocum? Or I have coffee."

Slocum noticed the wood stove, felt its heat. There was a pot of coffee sitting atop the firebox, steam rising from its spout. The coffee smelled strong.

"I'll skip both the coffee and the whiskey," Slocum said.

"Alexis?" Chadwick asked.

"Nothing for me either, Luke."

Chadwick walked over to the bed and slid a strongbox out from underneath. He opened the box and took out a stack of currency. He brought the money over to the table and set it down in front of Slocum.

"That," Chadwick said, "is the money I owe you for the mules you brought out from Missouri. That is the full amount for the price we agreed upon when I contracted you to bring the mules out to me. I regret that my men were dishonest and attempted to take your mules without paying for them."

"You didn't know anything about Beddoes and Deakins stealing those mules?" Slocum asked.

"I swear," Chadwick said. "They acted on their own."

"They also killed my partner, Tad Foster."

"I deeply regret that."

"That's also a debt," Slocum said. "And, if those men were in your employ, then you must assume responsibility not only for the theft of my mules, but for the murder of an innocent young man."

Chadwick reached into his pocket and pulled out a

long, slim wallet. He counted out a number of bills and laid these on the table as he sat down.

"What's that?" Slocum asked as Chadwick slid the bills toward Slocum.

"That, Slocum, represents burial expenses for your partner and a week's wages in advance if you'll come to work for me."

"Doing what?" Slocum asked.

"Nothing real hard," Chadwick said. "I'm going to need an extra man when I move some wagons down the hill. I want to make sure nobody tries to rob me."

"You mean you want me to work as a hired gun," Slocum said.

"Well, that's a crude way of putting it. I hear you're a pretty good man with a gun."

"Where'd you hear that?"

"Well, you do have a reputation, you know."

"I thought a man's private life was private."

"Isn't the law looking for you down in Georgia? Maybe in some other places, too?"

"I don't believe that's any of your business, Chadwick."

"No, it's not, and I don't hold it against you. Now, how about my offer?"

Slocum picked up the stack of bills that Chadwick had set on the table first. He fanned through them, counting the twenty dollar bills. He put the bills inside his shirt, right behind his belly gun.

"There's that other stack, Slocum," Chadwick said.

Alexis ran her tongue across her lower lip as the two men stared at each across the table.

"I don't want burying money for Tad Foster," Slocum said. "And I don't need a job."

"I'm paying good money for a little bit of work and for a short time," Chadwick said.

Slocum pushed his chair back away from the table and stood up. He looked down at Chadwick. "The money may be good," he said, "but I'm not interested in working for you. And as for the money you paid for the mules, that isn't all of the debt that's owed."

"What do you mean? I paid you in full for those mules."

"I'm talking about Tad Foster, a kid who never did anyone any harm. A kid who had his whole life to look forward to. A kid who was a better man than those two who took his life away. That's a debt I aim to see paid. A life for a life, Chadwick."

"If you have proof . . ."

"Are you talking about me going to the law up here in Belleville, Chadwick?"

"Why, yes. I certainly would want to see justice done. Just like you."

Alexis watched the two men, her eyes glittering. Slocum could almost feel the passion rising up in her.

"I doubt I'd find justice up here in Holcomb Valley," Slocum said.

"You should report your friend's death to our constable, Sid Lawton."

"I've met Lawton," Slocum said. "And he looks to me like a man who bends the law to suit himself."

"Sid Lawton is an honorable man."

"Hmm. You could have fooled me," Slocum said. "This morning, I saw a girl who had been murdered, stabbed to death, cut up like some animal and left to die."

"I know nothing about that," Chadwick said.

"No? Well, let me ask you this," Slocum said. "Does a man called Little Bill work for you?"

Chadwick's face turned an ashen gray. He blinked and Slocum saw beads of sweat rise in one of the furrows creasing Chadwick's forehead.

"Little Bill? I-I don't believe I know the name," Chadwick said.

Slocum knew he was lying.

"I saw Little Bill and Alexis ride up here yesterday, hell-bent-for-leather. After that girl was killed, I saw Little Bill sneak off all covered with blood. I tracked him to Union Flat. Your constable was right there, too, watching while Little Bill washed the blood out of his shirt. And guess who was also there? Your men, Beddoes and Deakins, all cozied up in camp like a kinfolk reunion.

"So, don't tell me about justice here in Holcomb Valley or pretend you don't know what the hell's going on, Chadwick. I figure you're in this up to your neck and that money there is just your way of buying me off."

"Slocum, you're seven kinds of sonofabitch, you know that? Take your damned money and get the hell out of here."

Slocum looked at Alexis. He smiled. "Does that mean I don't get a buggy ride back to town?"

"Get out," Chadwick shouted. "You can walk to hell for all I care."

Alexis sat there, frozen in her chair.

"Thanks for paying me what you owe, Chadwick," Slocum said. "I'll be seeing you, bye and bye."

"Good riddance," Chadwick spluttered.

For a moment, Slocum thought Chadwick was going to stand up and go for his pistol, but by the time he reached the door, he knew Chadwick was too much a coward to draw down on a man who was facing him.

As he walked out the door, Slocum figured out what kind of man Chadwick was. He hired men to kill for him. But when he starting walking back toward town, he kept looking over his shoulder.

For, if he figured right, Chadwick was the kind who would shoot a man in the back.

And that kind of man, Slocum knew, was a man to watch.

18

The ride to Pygmy Cabin took less than a half hour from Octagon House. Lucy led the way on her horse just as the long shadows of afternoon began to darken and the sun began to sink behind the San Bernardino Mountains.

"There it is," Lucy said, pointing to what looked, at first glance, like a jumble of deadfalls, logs stacked atop each other.

As they drew close, Slocum saw that the logs were rough-hewn with an axe and formed a squat, small structure. He tried to imagine what it must have been like for the prospector who had to build the cabin in order to save his life before winter froze him in. He wondered if the man had survived in such a small dwelling.

"I think I see a note," Lucy said.

"No sign of your friend, Betsy," Slocum said.

"John, I'm terribly worried."

"I'll get the note," he said. "You stay on your horse just in case we have to leave in a hurry."

Slocum swung down out of the saddle and walked over

to the note pinned to one of the logs with a rusty, square nail.

"Uh oh," he said.

"What's wrong?" Lucy asked.

"This is not good news, Lucy."

"R-read it to me," she stammered.

"All right. Brace yourself. The note says: 'IF YOU WANT TO SEE BETSY ALIVE, SLOCUM, YOU AND THE BANCROFT WOMAN GET OUT OF BELLE-VILLE BY TOMORROW.' "

"Oh, my, they've got Betsy," Lucy exclaimed.

"It looks that way. But who? And where do they have her?"

He walked over to Lucy's horse and handed her the note. She read it twice and tears welled up in her eyes.

"It's my fault. I never should have brought Betsy into this. Now, she's a prisoner and her friend, and mine, Constance, is dead. What have I done?"

"It's not your fault, Lucy. The problem now is what do we do about it?"

"Why, we'll have to leave Belleville, that's all."

Slocum pulled a cheroot from his pocket and walked back to his horse. He checked the sawed-off Greener wrapped in a blanket that was tied in back of the cantle. It was snug, but would pull free very easily. He lit the cheroot and drew smoke through it as he thought of this latest setback.

"That's just what Chadwick and his bunch want us to do," Slocum said. "And that won't guarantee Betsy's free-dom. In fact, if you confided in her, she knows too much. They'll kill her to cover their tracks, just like they did with your father and Constance."

Lucy gasped as the weight of Slocum's words struck her. "You're right, of course. But what can we do? We don't even know where they're keeping Betsy. And there's just the two of us. How can we stand up to Chadwick and his bunch?"

"Do you know a miner named Sam Coberly?"

"I know who he is. He and his three sons keep pretty much to themselves. My father knew him, though, and I think he admired him."

"Well, he's offered to help. I think we may need some extra hands with this."

"It's going to be dark soon. There's not much we can do once that sun goes down."

"I think there is," Slocum said. "First thing we're going to do is check out of the hotel and tell the clerk we're going to San Bernardino."

"What good will that do?" she asked.

"We'll start out that way, but double back to Union Flat. We'll have our bedrolls and food with us, so we'll camp out tonight as if we were on the trail to San Bernardino. I'll cover our tracks. My guess is that by morning, Chadwick will think we're gone. As matter of fact, he will probably think that tonight. I imagine he has spies all over Belleville."

"Yes, I'm sure someone will tell him that we're gone."

"Good, let's get to it, then. Unless you'd rather not come along with me."

"John, I wouldn't miss this for anything. I want to see Betsy again. Alive. I want to give her a great big hug."

"Okay, let's go back to the hotel and get our gear together and check out."

"Yes, let's," she said.

An hour later, Lucy and Slocum, for all appearances, were heading toward Big Bear Lake and the twisting road that led down to San Bernardino. Slocum had Tad's horse on a rope and was leading him. The people who saw them going would think, he was sure, that they were leaving Belleville. And some of them probably knew why.

Shadows began to stretch across the road out of Belleville and the valley behind them darkened quickly once the sun sank below the high peaks of the muscular San Bernardino Mountains. In the distance, the high, domed peak of San Gorgonio, still white-capped, shone with the last golden rays of the sun.

"We don't want to go too far down this road," Slocum said, "and I hope you can guide me when we double back. I want to circle Holcomb Valley and come up on the other side of Union Flat."

"I know the valley well," Lucy said. "And I can guide you where we have to go. As a matter of fact, we'll come very close to where my father had his mine."

Slocum checked his back trail and saw no sign that they were being followed. When the road made a dip, he turned to the right, taking them off the trail and into the trackless pine forest.

"This is a good place," Lucy said. "You picked it well. We can circle wide through here. If you look through the trees, you can see the lights along Big Bear Lake. Some people have already lit their lamps."

Slocum looked down the slope and saw golden reflections of lamps on the waters of the lake. And beyond, through the pines, he saw lamplit windows, just barely visible in the clear mountain air.

"It's beautiful down there," Lucy said. "My father and

I used to ride out here and just look at the lake and the lights in the evenings. It gave him comfort."

"I can see why," Slocum said and then turned his horse up the slope at an angle, taking them well away from the road. He rode slowly so that he did not make noise that any tracker could hear.

"I should take the lead from now on," Lucy said. "My horse knows this country and it will be pitch black soon."

"Just be careful," Slocum said, "and go slow and quiet."

"Just follow me," Lucy said.

The darkness increased as Lucy and Slocum rode back up to Holcomb Valley. Slocum was satisfied that no one was following them and by the time they reached the rock outcroppings that dotted the outer edge of the valley, he was sure of it.

He began to recognize landmarks as the moon rose. Lucy stopped behind a large pile of rocks that he did not recognize, however.

"Coberly's's cabin is right down there," she said. "Can you see the light from his lamps?"

Slocum leaned down over the pommel of his saddle. He saw the splash of yellow-orange light on the ground. That's when he also noticed the silence.

"I see the cabin," Slocum said. "Did you notice the blasting that we've heard all day long has stopped?"

"Yes, I just now noticed it. I've never heard so much dynamiting before up here."

"Let's ride down there. I hope one of Sam's boys doesn't shoot us."

"So do I," Lucy said.

"Hello, the cabin," Slocum called as they drew near.

"John, is that you?" called Sam.

"Yes. I'm here with Lucy Bancroft."

"Ride on down."

Slocum heard voices and the creak of a door. When he and Lucy rode into the light, Sam was standing there with two of his boys. All had rifles in their hands and wore gun belts. It was a hell of a way to live, Slocum thought.

"What brings you out so late, John?" Sam asked.

"I need your help."

"Trouble?"

"A heap of it," Slocum said, stepping down out of the saddle. He helped Lucy dismount and Sam ushered them into his cabin. The boys stared at Lucy as if she were an apparition.

"You're just in time for supper," Sam said.

"Maybe we should eat something," Lucy said.

"Good. Set the folks a chair, Steve," Sam said. "Brad, you put the vittles on for Cap'n John and Miss Bancroft."

"Where's your other boy?" Slocum asked.

"Jesse's out scoutin'. Might be what he's lookin' for is what you're lookin' for," Sam said.

"My friend, Betsy, you know, the one who works at the dining hall at Octagon House, has been kidnapped," Lucy said.

"I've seen her a time or two. Nice blond gal, pretty eyes."

"I'm very worried about her," Lucy said.

"Do you know anything that might help us find her?" Slocum asked.

Steve began setting bowls and pots on the table, while Brad set out extra plates, knives, forks and spoons. The boys were quiet about it. There was none of the usual clatter and Slocum knew that they, and their father, were listening for any sound from outside. He noticed that Coberly had latched and bolted the door with a reinforced two-by-four. There were rifle ports in the walls, too. Curtains shielded the sleeping rooms from view. Steve took the lid off a steaming pot of stew and Brad opened another filled with boiled potatoes.

"Venison," Sam said. "Dig in, you two."

"About that information," Slocum said.

"Well, Brad here saw a lot of comings and goings this afternoon after you left, John. And Chadwick was blasting so much, we shut down work in our mine. I didn't want to risk having the boys inside in case there was a cave-in."

"So, what about these comings and goings?" Slocum asked, as Lucy ladled food onto his plate.

"I sent each of the boys off to see what was going on," Sam said. "Brad went over to the place where you saw Little Bill, Beddoes, Deakins and that whole bunch. Steve went over to their cabin, and Jesse and I moseyed over to where they were blasting."

"And what did you see or hear at these places, Sam?"

"Something's sure as hell goin' on up here. Chadwick's got six wagons all lined up and hitched to the mules you brought out from Missouri. Little Bill and Beddoes rode off and only Beddoes came back, talking about Little Bill having Betsy in his cabin. And that blasting, which I thought was Chadwick going into a hill and chunkin' out a mine shaft wasn't that at all."

"What was it?"

"Near as I can figure, Chadwick's closing up all the mines he stole or filed on, shuttin' 'em plumb down."

"Why?"

"I don't know," Sam said.

"Do you know where Little Bill's cabin is?" Slocum asked.

"Lucy knows right where it is," Sam said. "It's where she and her pa lived when he was alive."

"Our cabin? That's where Little Bill took Betsy?" Lucy asked.

"That's what Beddoes was sayin'. It don't look none too good for that gal Betsy. I don't know if you remember, Lucy, but a couple of years ago, some woman claimed Little Bill jumped her and violated her."

"I remember that," Lucy said. "There was a lot of talk, but Little Bill got off. The judge said it was her word against Little Bill's."

"Well, he done it more'n once," Sam said. "I heard he liked to be rough with the ladies, even them he paid for."

Lucy gasped.

Slocum's eyes narrowed and a muscle twitched in his jaw. He and Lucy stopped eating for a minute and looked at each other.

"John," she said, "we've got to . . ."

"I know. We'll have to rescue Betsy before Little Bill . . ."

He let his words trail off. Sam cleared his throat and swallowed the venison in his mouth.

"I figured the gal came willing," Sam said, "so I didn't think much of it at the time. But, now I remember why they call that jasper Little Bill. It ain't polite and I ain't goin' to say what it is in front of Miss Lucy here. But, John, another part of him is what he calls 'Big Bill.' And that's what he uses on the women."

Slocum pushed his plate away and stood up.

"We'll be back, Sam. You know where we're going."

"I reckon to get that gal Betsy away from Little Bill," Sam said.

"And away from Big Bill," Slocum said.

19

Betsy Carmichael trembled with fear.

She lay spread-eagle on her back atop the bed that her friend Lucy used to sleep in. Little Bill finished tying her left leg to the bedpost. Her other leg and wrists had already been tied so tightly, it hurt.

"Little Bill, please," she pleaded. "Don't hurt me."

Little Bill's eyes glittered like a snake's in the moonlight. He smelled of whiskey and sweat and he had touched her in private places where no man had touched her before, both when he had grabbed her at Pygmy Cabin and after Beddoes had left and he threw her onto the bed.

"Betsy, dearie, you're going to tell me everything that Lucy Bancroft told you and tell me where you put the papers she gave you."

"I-I don't know what you're talking about."

"Yes, you do. I know that Lucy gave you some papers and that you hid them away somewhere. Now, either you're going tell me, or you'll be mighty sorry."

"I-I can't," Betsy said.

"Suit yourself. Let's start with your shoes and stockings."

Little Bill pulled off Betsy's shoes and then stripped her stockings down both legs. He threw them on the floor.

"Are you going to tell me now?" he asked.

Betsy, her lips pressed tightly together, shook her head.

Little Bill drew a knife from the sheath on his belt and Betsy's eyes went wide in fear. He stepped close to her and grabbed the bodice of her dress. With the blade of his knife, he began to slit the dress from neck to navel in a slow, deliberate stroke as Betsy squirmed atop the bed.

"Stop it," she screamed.

"Nobody can hear you out here," Little Bill said. "Are you going to talk to me?"

"No. Leave me alone. Go away."

Little Bill laughed and slit the dress asunder, clear to the hem, exposing Betsy's panty-clad loins. He kneeled down with one leg on the bed and pushed his face close to hers, the knife clutched in his hand so that she could see it.

"I'll bet you have real purty breasts," he said, his breath hot and steamy against her face.

Betsy turned her head away from Little Bill. He laughed again and reached down and cupped one of her breasts in his hand. Her brassiere stretched taut as she tried to wriggle away from his grasp. But it was hopeless. She was tightly bound to the bed. She could only avoid looking at her attacker. Little Bill squeezed the breast as if testing a piece of fruit.

"Stop it. That's not funny," Betsy said.

"If you want me to stop, gal, all you gotta do is tell me what I want to know."

"I'll never tell you anything," Betsy said, pulling on both her arms in an attempt to free herself.

"Let's just see, dearie," Little Bill said. He brought the knife down to the center of Betsy's bra and lifted it with his left hand, then slid the knife blade underneath. Then, he ripped upward with the blade, severing the bra in two. The covering fell away like two cloth cups, exposing her breasts. Betsy gasped in alarm, trying instinctively to cover them with her hands, which were tied tightly at the wrists to the bedposts.

"You evil man," Betsy spat.

Little Bill bent down and kissed first one breast, then the other.

"You do have a pair of beauties," he said. "Prettiest I ever seen, maybe."

"How dare you?" Betsy exclaimed as Little Bill wallowed one of the nipples in his mouth. Despite herself, the nipple grew hard as a corn kernel as Little Bill licked it with his tongue.

"I'll bet that feels real good, girlie," Little Bill said, his voice turning husky as he became aroused.

He moved his mouth to the other breast and began to run his tongue around the nipple and to suck on it as Betsy squirmed to try and avoid his indecency.

That nipple, too, became hard as an acorn as Little Bill slobbered over it, pulling on it with his teeth and licking the nubbin with relish.

"Stop it," Betsy cried. "Please stop doing that."

"Oh, I'll stop, all right, sweet Betsy from Pike. As soon as you tell me where you got those papers Miss Lucy Bancroft gave to you."

"I-I can't tell you," Betsy lied. "I don't know."

"Damn you, we'll see about that," Little Bill said and rose up, brandishing the knife once again. He looked down at her panties and Betsy cringed as if to escape from his lustful gaze.

"Them has got to come off," Little Bill said, and touched the top of her panties with the knife tip.

"D-don't, please," Betsy pleaded. "Don't you have a shred of decency in you?"

"Nary," Little Bill said, and sliced through the thin silken cloth with the knife. He cut the panties away, grabbed them and threw them in Betsy's face. She lifted her head and the shredded panties slipped to her neck.

"Now, ain't that a pretty sight," Little Bill said.

"You beast," Betsy said, twisting and writhing, pulling on the ropes that bound her.

Little Bill began unbuckling his gun belt. He dropped his pants and climbed onto the bed, straddling Betsy. He spread her legs a little wider and slid higher over her body.

"Don't," Betsy said.

Little Bill slapped her on the mouth. "You hush now," he said.

He entered her brutally, thrusting his cock into her cunt even as she squirmed to avoid this invasion. Little Bill sighed as he stabbed deep into her cunt. He began to pump back and forth, up and down, as Betsy writhed and wriggled. This only served to excite Little Bill more and he increased the tempo of his strokes.

Betsy screamed in protest, but Little Bill ignored her. "This is what you get when you don't tell me what I want to know," he said, in rhythm with his thrusting.

"You-you . . ." Betsy said and closed her eyes.

Little Bill pumped in and out, his cock swollen to an enormous size. He laid down his knife and grabbed her hips and pulled them up so that he could plumb her deeper. The bed creaked and moaned with the weight of the two people.

"Nice, nice," Little Bill said. "Tight, the way I like it."

"Stop, please stop!" Betsy screamed.

"You don't talk, sissy, you pay the price."

"I hate you," she said.

"Oh, you hate me, but you're givin' me a lot of lovin', gal."

Little Bill savagely thrust his cock even deeper and Betsy cried out in pain. She made her body as stiff as she could, but this did not stop Little Bill from giving her all he had. He doubled up a fist and smashed her in the mouth.

"Loosen up," he said.

But Betsy stiffened her legs even more. Despite herself, she became aroused and yet she didn't want him to know that she was excited and she closed her eyes and clamped her lips together tightly.

"That's good, you're squeezin', gal. Makes it all the better."

Betsy suddenly relaxed to lessen Little Bill's pleasure and she saw his eyes burn with rage. He slapped her mouth until a tiny trickle of blood began to seep from one corner.

"Get smart, now," Little Bill said, "and you'll pay a dear price, sis."

Frantic now, Betsy began to scream at the top of her lungs as Little Bill continued to bore into her cunt with ever more brutal strokes.

Little Bill slapped Betsy's face until it was red and was just about to explode his balls into her when he heard the front door slam open. He heard footsteps pounding on the pineboard floor and quickly slid from Betsy's body.

"Who in hell is that?" Little Bill called as he pulled his pants back up his legs.

There was no answer.

"Help, help!" Betsy screamed.

"You shut up," Little Bill said as he stooped to pick up his gun belt.

"We're coming," someone yelled and Little Bill knew it was a woman's voice. He strapped on his gun belt and drew his pistol.

"He's got a gun!" Betsy screamed.

Little Bill whirled on her, bringing up his pistol to shoot her.

But he was too late. The door to the bedroom burst open and a tall man in a black frock coat filled the door frame.

"Drop it, Little Bill," Slocum said. He held his Colt in his hand. Behind him, Lucy Bancroft tried to peer into the room.

"Damn you, Slocum."

Little Bill swung his pistol to bear on Slocum, but he was too late.

Slocum squeezed the trigger and the Colt bucked in his hand. Little Bill staggered backward as the bullet caught in the center of his chest. Then he started to pitch forward as he tried to regain his balance. His pistol fired and the bullet dug a furrow in the floor, spitting up splinters. He crumpled up then and sprawled to the floor on his face, blood gushing from the hole in his chest. The pistol fell from his grasp as he turned over.

"Damn you," Little Bill said again.

"No, Little Bill, it's you who are damned," Slocum said.

Lucy rushed to the bed and clasped Betsy in her arms. Betsy began sobbing and soon Lucy was sobbing, too.

"You got me good, Slocum," Little Bill gasped. "Damn your rebel hide."

"You'd better save what little breath you got left," Slocum said, "and say a prayer."

"I-I . . ." Little Bill started to say, but he couldn't finish it. He let out a long gasp and could not draw another breath. He shuddered once, twice, and then twitched a last time. His eyes closed and he lay still, no longer bleeding, no longer breathing.

Slocum turned to the bed to see Lucy embracing a naked Betsy. He slid his Colt back into its holster. The barrel was still smoking slightly. He saw the ripped clothing lying around the bed and began to pick them up.

"Better untie her, Lucy," Slocum said. "We've still got a lot to do."

"Betsy, did he hurt you bad?" Lucy asked tearfully.

Betsy nodded.

"He won't hurt you anymore," Slocum said, handing Lucy the items of clothing he had picked up off the floor.

"Turn your back, John," Lucy said. "Betsy's not decent yet."

Slocum walked back over to Little Bill and nudged his side with the toe of his boot. Satisfied that Little Bill was dead, he picked up the man's pistol and shoved it in his waistband. He walked out of the room, fishing for a cheroot in his pocket.

He was glad they had gotten there when they did because he was sure that Little Bill would have killed Betsy when he was through using her. Slocum had seen his kind before.

He struck a match and lit his cheroot.

"Hurry up, Lucy," Slocum called as he walked to the front door. "We don't have much time."

He knew there was still a lot to do. Chadwick was up to something and there was still that debt to pay. Beddoes and Deakins still owed for taking the life of Tad Foster.

Slocum meant to see that they paid the debt in full.

20

On the ride back to Coberly's cabin, Slocum had the chance to question Betsy about her kidnapping. She wore clothing that Lucy had given her, from garments that were still in the Bancroft house.

"Did you hear anything at all about Chadwick's plans?" Slocum asked.

"The only thing I heard that might help you," Betsy said, "was when Beddoes rode off, leaving me alone with Little Bill."

Betsy was still badly shaken from her ordeal and her voice quavered with emotion. She was riding Lucy's horse. Lucy was riding Little Bill's.

"What was that?" Slocum asked.

"Beddoes said, 'I'll see you later down at Whiskey Springs.' "

"Did you take that to mean tonight?"

"Yes. Little Bill said he'd be there in a couple of hours."

"I wonder what's going on down there," Lucy said.

"So do I," Slocum replied.

"Lucy," Betsy said, "I didn't tell Little Bill anything. I mean where you hid the evidence or any of that."

"What is this evidence you have, Lucy?" Slocum asked.

"I suppose there's no reason to keep it from you any longer, John."

"You mean you didn't trust me before?"

"I guess I have learned not to trust very many people. But I trust you, John."

"Will the evidence you have do any good to bring Chadwick and his bunch to justice?" Slocum asked.

"I think so," Lucy said. "I went over the ground where my father was killed and made plaster casts of the hoof-prints of the horses. I also have the rope that was around my father's neck. And I have statements from witnesses who saw my father killed."

"Why didn't you take the evidence to a lawman or a judge?" Slocum asked.

"Because I knew Sid Lawton was in on it. Betsy over-heard him planning it with Chadwick, and another waiter heard it, too. I have all those statements and I matched the plaster casts with two horses, one belonging to Bed-does, the other to Deakins."

"Where did you put all this evidence?"

"Should I tell him, Betsy?"

"Yes, Lucy, you should."

"Near Pygmy Cabin," Lucy said, "there is one of the stumps left there when the prospector cut down trees for that cabin. It's hollow. I put everything in there, the pa-pers in a strongbox and the plasters wrapped in heavy oilcloth to preserve them. You can't tell by looking at the stump that there's anything in it."

"And, it's all still there," Betsy said. "No one has even been near it."

"So that's why you were at Pygmy Cabin," Slocum said.

"Yes," Betsy said.

"And you're sure no one saw you looking at that stump."

"I'm sure," Betsy said.

"Well, that evidence may help someday," Slocum said. "But we already know we can't trust Lawton. He's in with Chadwick and as crooked as that whole bunch."

"Yes, John," Lucy said. "Now you can see what I've been up against."

The lamps were still lit at Coberly's cabin when Slocum, Lucy and Betsy rode up. A grim-faced Sam greeted them as they rode up.

"Best light down," Sam said. "There's big trouble. I see you're riding Little Bill's horse, Betsy. Did you steal it from him?"

"Little Bill is dead," Slocum said.

"Good riddance."

Slocum swung down out of the saddle. He helped Betsy dismount. She was still trembling and by the way she lowered her head, he could tell she was ashamed about what had happened to her at the hands of Little Bill.

"There's no need to be ashamed," Slocum told her. "None of what happened was your fault, Betsy. Little Bill is not worth blaming yourself over. He got what he deserved."

"I know," Betsy said, "but I can't stop thinking about it. It was so awful."

Lucy patted Betsy on the back and put her arms around

her. "John's right, Betsy. Come on inside and have a cup of coffee."

"Coffee's on," Sam said. "But I'm afraid Jesse's been hurt. Brad and Steve are looking after him."

As they walked inside the cabin, Steve met them. Sam told him to keep a lookout and Steve went outside, carrying a rifle.

"I'll keep my eyes open, Pa," Steve said.

Inside the cabin, Jesse was sitting on a chair, his shirt off. Brad was daubing some strong-smelling liniment or ointment on a wound in his shoulder.

"Jess," Sam said, "tell Cap'n John what you saw down at Union Flat."

"Yes, sir," Jesse said.

"Did you get shot?" Slocum asked.

"Just a scratch, Cap'n."

"Do you know who shot you?"

"Yes, sir, it was Beddoes, with that damned Greener of his'n. One of the pellets got me in the shoulder. I lit out quick."

"Anybody follow you?"

"Nope. They was in too much of a hurry to get them wagons movin'."

"They were moving the wagons?" Slocum asked.

"Yep. They had three of 'em, and four mules to a wagon, which was kind of puzzlin', 'cause they wasn't nothin' in any of 'em."

"What?" Slocum asked.

"That's why I circled around, to see where was they goin'. I follered 'em plumb to Yucca Flat and then I high-tailed it back home to tell Pa."

"I don't know where Yucca Flat is," Slocum said.

Lucy stepped up then and put a hand on Slocum's shoulder. "He's talking about that flat across from Whiskey Springs."

"Yeah, they was a bunch of 'em down there, with torches, drinkin' and hollering and diggin' out in the flat."

"Tell Cap'n Slocum who-all it was you saw goin' down there, Jess."

Brad stepped away from Jesse and Slocum saw there were two small holes in the flesh of Jesse's shoulder. The wounds did not appear to be serious, but the boy would have a sore shoulder for a time.

"Well, besides Beddoes and Deakins, I seen Chadwick and the constable, Lawton, and Weed, the sheriff down at Victor, and some other men."

"What's down in Yucca Flat?" Slocum asked Sam.

"Ain't nothin' down there that I know of," Sam said. "There sure as hell isn't any gold, less'n someone planted it there."

Slocum swore. "I think that's exactly what they did," Slocum said.

"Huh?" Sam blinked in surprise.

"When Lucy and I passed by there, I noticed a lot of wagon tracks and signs of digging. Maybe Chadwick has been caching gold on Yucca Flat. And maybe that's why he needed all those mules. If the wagons left here empty, they were going someplace to get filled up. Four mules on a team can haul a lot of gold."

"You know," Sam said, "that explains a lot of things."

"Like what?" Slocum asked.

"There have been riders coming and going from that camp on the flat here at all hours of the night."

"You know that blasting you've been hearing?" Jesse asked Slocum.

Slocum nodded.

"Well, I found out today what it was all about. Chadwick's men haven't been blasting new shafts in the mountains here. They've been closing up mines they stole."

"I'll bet I know why," Lucy said.

"Why?" Slocum asked.

"People have been disappearing up here all the time," she said. "I'll bet there are dead bodies in all those mines they closed up."

"So," Slocum said, "it looks as if Chadwick and Lawton have played out their hand. They're fixing to leave Holcomb Valley and destroy all the evidence of their crimes."

"And they're probably taking a hell of a lot of gold with them," Sam said.

"We've got to stop them!" Lucy exclaimed.

Slocum and Sam looked at her. Betsy started to shake her head.

"Not you, Lucy," Slocum said. "You and Betsy had better stay here and get some sleep. Sam, if it's all right with you . . ."

"Why, sure," Sam said. "Me and the boys can go with you down to Whiskey Springs."

"And face all those men?" Lucy asked.

"They won't be expecting us," Slocum said.

"No, and they'll be busy digging up their cache," Sam said. "We ought to be able to even up the odds, eh, Cap'n?"

"I'd say we stand a good chance to catch Chadwick red-handed."

"I want to go, too," Jesse said. "My arm's okay. Pa?"

"If you're able," Sam said.

Jesse stood up and walked across the room. He took a clean shirt out of a wardrobe and began putting it on.

"Any way we can surprise them without riding right into them?" Slocum asked.

Sam scratched his head. He looked at Brad. Brad shrugged.

"Likely they'd be expecting us to ride the road down from Holcomb Valley," Sam said. "But, if we was to come up at 'em from the desert side, they'd be plumb surprised, I reckon."

"Pa, are you talking about that old trail we seen over yonder?" Brad asked.

"We could do it, I reckon," Sam said.

Slocum's face was a blank. He looked at Sam and Brad as Jesse walked over, buttoning his shirt.

"I know that place, Pa," Jesse said. "It's steep, but it comes out just below Whiskey Springs, right below that bluff above it."

"That's the place," Sam said. "Be mighty dangerous in the dark, though."

"I know the place you're talking about," Lucy said. "It's very dangerous at night. And that trail hasn't been used in years."

"Maybe you'd better tell me about it, Sam," Slocum said.

"Lucy knows about this," Sam said, "because her pa was one of the first settlers up here. Years ago, before they blasted any roads up into Holcomb Valley, the first prospectors and settlers had to drive stakes into the mountain to get their wagons up and down. They would wrap heavy ropes around the stakes and let out a little at time when they were going down to the desert. Or, when they came up here, they winched the wagons up the steep sides of the mountain."

"And one of those places is still here?" Slocum asked.

"More than one. But, if you noticed the bluff at Whiskey Springs and the side of the mountain, it takes a long slope on the other side of the bluff. That was one of the places."

"Ever hear of Liver-Eating Johnson?" Lucy asked Slocum.

"Yes. An old mountain man."

"He's supposed to buried somewhere on Yucca Flat, right across from Whiskey Springs. My father told me he was one of the men who told the flatlanders how to get their wagons up and down to Holcomb Valley from the desert side."

"Well, let's go down that way," Slocum said. "If you can find it in the dark, Sam."

"I can find it," Sam said.

"What about Steve, Pa?" Brad asked. "Is he coming with us?"

"We won't need him," Lucy said. "I can shoot."

"If you think you and Betsy will be all right," Sam said.

Betsy nodded and so did Lucy. "We'll be fine. Besides, it looks like Chadwick and Lawton are down at Whiskey Springs with all the rest of that bunch."

"Let's head out, then," Sam said. "Brad, go tell Steve he's comin' with us. Saddle up."

In a few moments, Slocum, Sam and his three boys were riding away from the Coberly cabin, Betsy and Lucy waving good-bye. The men heard the door slam when they rode out of sight.

"It's mighty quiet up here tonight," Sam said.

"It won't be quiet for long," Slocum said as he checked his rifle, both pistols and made sure his Greener was snug in his bedroll. The moon was up and cast a deathly pale coating of soft silver on the trees and earth as they rode toward the rim of Holcomb Valley, to a place Sam knew of, just below Whiskey Springs.

21

Slocum was the first to see the torches blazing down on Yucca Flat. He was riding just behind Sam Coberly, who was in the lead, picking his way through the darkness along an old trail that was just below the ridgeline overlooking the flat and Whiskey Springs.

"Do you see them down there, Sam?" Slocum asked.

"I can smell 'em."

"They've got the wagons lined up and are digging something up. They look like a pack of grave robbers."

"We'll be down in their midst soon. The next slope ahead is where we'll go down to the road."

In the moonlight, Slocum could see the wide path that the old wagoneers had used to come up and down. Young new growth had sprung up, but the road was visible and he could even make out the wagon ruts.

"How do we get down?" Slocum asked. "It looks pretty steep."

"It is steep," Sam whispered. "But the stakes are still there. We can either go straight down, using our ropes to keep us from picking up too much speed, or we can take longer and ride down like it was a switchback."

"You call it," Slocum said.

When they got to the sloping precipice, Sam beckoned to his sons and they rode up slow and quiet. "Shake out those ropes, Brad," Sam said.

Sam, Steve and Jesse all had strong lariats tied to their saddle rings and they snaked them out as if they had experience. Sam rode down cautiously to the first iron stake and made a loop in the rope using a knot that would not slip. He put the loop over the stake.

"I'll go down first to show you how, John," Sam said. "You come next. The boys have done this before, just for fun."

"A man could break his neck having fun here," Slocum said.

Sam rode down, pulling on the rope to slow the horse and himself. Slocum followed the same procedure. Jesse went last. When he reached the next stake where the others were waiting, he worked the rope up the stake until the loop was free. The men followed the same procedure until they had used the last stake and were on level ground.

Sam followed a dim path that brought them to the road just below Whiskey Springs, where he stopped to talk to Slocum.

"Do you have a plan, John?" he asked.

"Yes, I've been thinking about it. We'll form a single line and ride around the edge of the flat, using the cover there. Each man will wind up a hundred and fifty feet apart, and at my signal, we'll sneak across the flat to get as close as we can to where Chadwick's doing his dig-

ging. We'll surround him on three sides. We'll be ready
to shoot from horseback, if they open fire on us. That
sound good to you?"

"I think it'll work. My boys are good shooters and they
can fire from horseback."

"You taught them well, Sam."

They rode single file up to the lower edge of Yucca
Flat. They could hear Chadwick and his men talking and
grunting as they loaded heavy sacks of processed gold and
ore onto the wagons.

Slocum saw the torches stuck in the ground, and the
three wagons. The extra mules were tied to the backs of
the wagons. None of the men he saw seemed to be on
guard. He figured they could ride pretty close to the edge
of the light cast by the torches before being spotted.

When all the others were in place, Slocum started riding
out from the edge of the flat toward the wagons and men
digging up their cache. He pulled the sawed-off shotgun
from his bedroll and checked that both barrels were
loaded. At close range, he knew, the double-barreled
Greener was a potent weapon.

Slocum rode a good hundred yards before anyone in
the circle of light saw him. He heard a shout and saw men
scrambling for their rifles. He kicked the Palouse in the
flanks and the horse broke into a fast gallop.

Out of the corner of his eye, Slocum saw Sam and
his sons galloping toward Chadwick and his men. He
hunched over the pommel of his saddle and cocked both
barrels of the shotgun.

One of Chadwick's bunch fired a shot. He heard the
bullet sizzle a foot over his head as his horse closed the
distance. Other shots rang out, and then Sam, Steve, Brad

and Jesse began shooting at the diggers, some of whom had taken refuge behind the wagons.

Slocum reined his horse hard over to the right so that he could flank those hiding behind the wagons and he hoped one of Sam's boys would do the same on the other side.

The firing picked up and bullets whined off of rocks that littered the flat. Slocum rode in close and saw a man rise up to shoot at Sam. He squeezed the first trigger of his shotgun and the weapon belched flame and lethal lead pellets.

"There's Slocum," Chadwick shouted. "Get him."

Slocum wheeled the Palouse just as a volley of rifle fire cracked ahead of him. He saw orange blossoms of flame spurt from two rifles. He fired the other barrel of his shotgun and saw one of the men throw up his arms and fall back, his body riddled with double-aught buckshot.

Quickly, Slocum pulled the Winchester from its sheath and rammed the Greener in the same scabbard. He jacked a shell into the chamber and pulled his horse to a halt.

Sid Lawton stepped out from behind the wagon, bringing his rifle up to his shoulder. Slocum fired from the hip, then kicked his horse in the flanks. Lawton fired and Slocum heard the bullet whistle past his ear.

Sam and his sons were all in close now and picking targets. They had the advantage since Chadwick and his men were backlit by the flaming torches. Slocum saw men go down as he fired his rifle rapidly to flush those hiding behind the wagons out into the open.

Slocum ran out of ammunition in the rifle. He reached back and stuck it inside his bedroll, then drew his Colt from its holster.

"Slocum," a man shouted.

Slocum turned and saw Beddoes standing ten yards away with a double-barreled shotgun aimed straight at him.

"I got you now," Beddoes said and lifted the shotgun to his shoulder.

"This is for Tad," Slocum said, squeezing the trigger of his pistol. The Colt bucked in his hand and he saw Beddoes drop the shotgun and claw at his chest. A bright red flower of blood bloomed on Beddoes's chest and he staggered in a small circle before falling down.

Deakins rushed toward Slocum, firing his pistol wildly. Slocum dropped him with a shot to the belly, then whirled his horse as he heard a sound close by, behind him.

Chadwick and Lawton stood side by side, both holding pistols aimed straight at Slocum.

"Drop it, Slocum," Chadwick said, "or we'll empty your saddle."

Slocum knew the two men had him cold. He started counting the number of shots he had used up with his pistol. He counted twice and the answer always the same.

He had one bullet left.

And he faced two deadly men, no more than ten feet away from him.

"Better do what Chad says, Slocum," Lawton said, "or you're wolf meat."

Slocum drew a breath and held it.

One shot. Two men. Both killers. Chadwick and Lawton.

The odds were all on their side, Slocum knew.

For a long moment, he was staring eternity square in the face.

22

It seemed to Slocum that everything had stopped stock-still. In those few pulse beats when he had to make a decision, he could no longer hear the sound of gunfire, nor was he aware of anything but the sound of his own heartbeat.

He heard the *swick-click* of a hammer cocking. Then another, as Chadwick and Lawton prepared to shoot him out of the saddle. And he knew he had only one shot left in his Colt six-gun. One shot for two deadly men.

"How many bullets do you have left in that six-shooter, Slocum?" Lawton asked, as he took deadly aim on Slocum from less than a dozen feet away.

"I think he's empty," Chadwick said, steadying his own pistol.

Slocum weighed his chances. He did not know either man, but he had to make a decision fast. Chadwick hired out his killings. Maybe Lawton did, too. But Lawton was a lawman and no doubt proficient with a pistol to a greater degree than Chadwick.

If he could only kill or disable one man, which should it be?

The seconds ticked by at a crawl.

Lawton was the one who made up Slocum's mind. Chadwick was licking his iips as if they had gone dry on him. Lawton stood steady as a rock. Chadwick had to steady his pistol once again.

Then, Slocum saw Lawton's trigger finger start to move.

Slocum leveled the Colt at his hip and squeezed off a shot at Lawton. Then he ducked and slid out of the saddle, keeping the Palouse between him and Chadwick.

No sooner did his feet hit the ground than Slocum holstered the empty Colt and slid the Greener out of its sheath. He fished two shells from his pocket, cracked the shotgun open, ejected the empty shells and crammed two new ones in. While he was doing this, he could hear two pistol shots, one a fraction of a second later than the first, and heard the buzz and whine of the bullets as they passed over his horse.

Slocum hit the underside of the barrels of the shotgun and stepped around the backside of the Palouse and cocked both hammers. As he did so, he saw Lawton twisting in agony, trying to stay on his feet. Chadwick's face was obscured by white smoke for a moment, but he was still standing.

Slocum saw Chadwick cock his single-action Remington and as he pulled the hammer back, Slocum stepped out, took aim, and fired off one barrel of the Greener.

Chadwick screamed as a full load of double-aught buckshot ripped into his midsection, smashing bones and flesh and piercing vital organs. Chadwick went down like a sack of meal.

Lawton gasped and tried to get off another shot at Slocum, despite his mortal wound.

Slocum let him have the second barrel at six feet and watched as Lawton's head came apart like a stack of dishes, pieces of his skull flying in all directions, his brains exploding to pulp amid a cloud of blood.

Sam rode up then, out of breath. He looked down at the two men, and then at Slocum, who was holding a smoking shotgun.

"We got 'em all, Cap'n," Sam said. "And you ought to see what's in them wagons."

"Ore?"

"You ain't goin' to believe what you see with your own eyes," Sam said.

"I'll take a look."

"Both of them are dead," Sam said, pointing his rifle at Chadwick and Lawton. "And you got Beddoes and that damned Deakins, too, I see."

Slocum walked over to the wagons. Two of them were filled with sacks of gold and some rich ore. Among the sacks of gold was something else, too. A large trunk. It was open.

"That's what I wanted you to see, Cap'n," Sam said, as his boys rode up and looked on.

Slocum reached in and pulled out banknotes and deeds. The banknotes were in large denominations and wrapped with twine. Stuck in the twine were pieces of paper with the name of the bank and the amounts in each bundle.

"What do you make of that, John?" Sam asked.

"Looks to me like Lawton and Chadwick opened up

the bank before they left, just for good measure."

"The town of Belleville's goin' to pin a medal on you when you bring back their money. Those bills were all deposited by hardworking, honest folk who live in Holcomb Valley."

"Is some of it yours?" Slocum asked.

Sam shook his head. "I don't trust no bank," he said.

"Well, Sam, you take it back and let them pin the medal on you. I'm going back to where I started out from."

"You ain't goin' to take none of the glory for this?"

"No," Slocum said.

"What about Miss Lucy? She's mighty sweet on you, I think."

"That's one of the reasons I'm not going back to Holcomb Valley," Slocum said. "But you can do me a favor, if you will."

"Anything," Sam said.

"Give her that horse of Tad's I left at your place. Tell her it's a parting gift from me."

"That it?" Sam asked.

Slocum walked over and shook Sam's hand. He waved to the boys, then walked over to his horse. He reloaded the Greener and shoved it back inside his bedroll. Then he shoved fresh cartridges into his Colt and reloaded the Winchester.

He turned and looked at the four men who had befriended him.

"Fellers," Slocum said, "there's a bottle of whiskey over across the road at Whiskey Springs. I'm going to have a drink and be on my way. I'd be mighty pleased if you'd join me. I don't have a bottle to leave in its place, but maybe you can replace it next time you're down this way."

Then Slocum climbed up on his horse and rode toward Whiskey Springs. When he looked back, he saw that Sam and his sons were following him.

Slocum's mouth began to water.

He looked back at Sam and grinned.

Watch for

HOT ON THE TRAIL

279th novel in the exciting SLOCUM series
from Jove

Coming in May!